Mail Order Maelstrom

Book 53 in Brides of Beckham

Kirsten Osbourne

Chapter One

Anabelle sat on the edge of the narrow bed she shared with her sisters, their three forms huddled together. Isabelle's eyes, usually brimming with a gentle light, were dulled by the weight of their reality. Rosabelle, ever the pillar, held her sisters' hands, her touch a feeble comfort against the chill that seeped through the thin floorboards.

Ana's gaze drifted to the window, the glass blurred with the remnants of past storms. Her fiery red hair, starkly contrasting to the drab surroundings, spilled over her shoulders untamed and wild. Each shout from their father that rose from downstairs punctured the quiet, and with every harsh syllable, her fists tightened. Knuckles white, she felt the simmering anger within her fighting for release, an inferno caged by circumstance.

Her jaw set, a silent rebellion against the timbers that groaned beneath the strain of their father's wrath. The man's voice, once a lullaby in her childhood memories, had become a herald of dread.

Izzy shivered beside her, and Rosie's grip grew firmer, a lifeline in the storm. Ana knew they could not weather this tempest much longer. This small room, swathed in sorrow and the residue of dreams deferred, could no longer contain the breadth of their yearning—a yearning for dawn after the darkest of nights.

Ana's whisper cut through the stifling silence, a strand of audacity against the backdrop of despair. "We must leave tonight," she murmured, her gaze burning into Izzy and Rosie's solemn faces. "There is nothing but sorrow for us here."

Her sisters' eyes, mirrors of her resolve, nodded mutely. With each word Ana spoke, a delicate blueprint of their escape unfurled in the dimness. She outlined the plan with precision. They would slip away into the night and venture beyond Beckham.

"Freedom awaits us," she promised.

In the corner of the room, a satchel lay open, its mouth gaping for the remnants of a life they would soon discard. Ana moved toward it. She reached first for the photograph, the image of their mother etched with sepia tones. A gentle touch traced the contours of the woman's smile before Ana nestled the photo amidst the sparse contents of the bag.

Next came the journal, its leather cracked with secrets and shared aspirations. Here lay the sketches of dreams. Within those scribbles, laughter and love lingered, a memory of how life was with their mother. Ana placed it atop the photograph, promising herself that they wouldn't give up on their dreams, even now, with their mother gone.

The bag was light. It bore the essence of three lives intertwined with all that the triplets had from their past.

"Time to go," Ana whispered, her grip on the satchel firm. She turned to her sisters, and together, they stepped toward the threshold into a life of freedom, no matter what hardships it may bring.

The wooden steps creaked under their weight. With each step they took, they worried their father would hear and his rage would be out of control once again. Ana firmly believed that if their mother hadn't been there to protect them, they all would have died as infants.

"Who's there?" he asked, more an accusation than a question.

Ana stilled, her hand reaching back to still Izzy and Rosie. She fixed her gaze on the shadows ahead, willing them to swallow the three of them whole.

"Quiet now," she mouthed to her sisters, the words a silent prayer. She took a step, then another, her movements deliberate.

She could feel Izzy and Rosie close behind her, their presence a heat at her back. Their eyes caught the scant light, wide orbs reflecting both the fear of what they fled and the anticipation of the freedom that beckoned just beyond the door.

"Girls?" The voice again, closer now.

Ana held her breath, pressing forward, the weight of years bearing down upon her slender shoulders. The darkness was a blanket around them, thick and suffocating, yet it was also a shield, helping them escape.

Ana's fingers found the cold metal of the doorknob, each heartbeat thundering in her ears a silent drumroll for the moment they had awaited. Behind them, their father's footsteps grew louder, and Ana said a silent prayer they would get away. All three of them had to escape together. They'd shared a womb, and they would share their lives. Their futures.

"Quickly," she urged.

Izzy and Rosie pressed close, a triad of trembling bodies yearning for the other side. The door's hinges groaned, a reluctant participant in their flight. Ana's grip tightened, knuckles white with the fear their father brought by merely being.

Then, the footsteps halted—a predator sensing its prey on the cusp of escape. Ana stilled, everything inside her begging her to move quickly. Each second seemed to take an eternity as they waited for just the right time to run.

A gush of cool night air embraced them, the scent of freedom mingling with the earthy aroma of the outside world. They stumbled out, the world suddenly vast and scary.

Their breaths came fast, misting in the air as if their very spirits sought to break free from the confines of their chests. The night wrapped around them, a cloak woven with threads of uncertainty and hope.

Ana led the charge, her red hair a fiery banner in the moon's pale light. It was done. Now they must run to the next town. Beckham. It meant freedom.

Ana's gaze cut through the gloom to find Izzy's, whose eyes shimmered with unshed tears, reflecting the starlight. So much had been endured in silence, so much pain held at bay by sheer will. Yet now, as their gazes locked, words were unnecessary. There was understanding—profound and complete. They were survivors, each scar a sign of their strength.

The night air, crisp and laden with the scent of pine, brushed against their skin, whispering of vast open spaces and possibilities. There were so many possibilities. They just had to get away from the farm to see them.

Ana led her sisters away from the silhouette of their childhood prison. Each step was a quiet rebellion, each breath a taste of liberty. The unpaved path beneath their feet crumbled like the remnants of a life they wished to forget.

As they reached the edge of town, they drew in a collective breath of relief. They'd made it this far. Now they had to make lives for themselves. They had money for train fare, and they'd go with no plan if they had to. The more distance between them and their father, the safer they would be.

"Look," Rosie murmured, her voice barely a thread in the fabric of the night. The candlelight beckoned, an ember of hope in the vast sea of their uncertainty.

Ana's fingers reached for her sisters', their grasp a silent oath. They were entwined, not just by blood, but by the shared resolve to create a different future for themselves. She felt the weight of their trust as she guided them toward the light.

They moved to the general store, each of them saying a silent prayer that they would find what they needed. A place to go. A future. They sat on the bench in front of the store, looking at one another, wondering what they should do next. They were near the train station, but they had to wait for the ticket office to open.

Hours later, they spotted a familiar face. Elizabeth Tandy had grown up on a farm near their father's, though they'd known her younger siblings better than her. When she saw the three of them there, she stopped.

"You're the Winslow triplets, right? You're the only triplets in the entire area. What are your first names?"

Ana smiled. "I'm Anabelle, and these are my sisters, Isabelle and Rosabelle."

"It's good to see you all again. I heard about your mother. I'm so sorry for your loss," Elizabeth said softly.

"Thank you," Ana replied.

"What are you all doing here in town?" Elizabeth asked. She knew the triplets were rarely allowed to go into town as well as everyone else in town did.

Ana looked at her sisters for a moment. "Our father is not a kind man. Mother kept us safe, but as you know..." Her voice trailed off. She couldn't yet admit out loud that their mother was dead. It hurt too much.

Elizabeth narrowed her eyes for a moment before nodding. "Come with me."

Rosie was the first to stand, but then Ana and Izzy followed suit. "Where?" Ana asked.

"To my home. I have an idea on how to keep the three of you safe. But I have a feeling being in the middle of town is a place your father will easily spot you."

Ana sighed. "We have money for train fares..." And they did. Mother had given them money from selling her wedding ring. She'd known she was going to die, and she said there was no reason they should die with her.

"Do you know where you'll go?" Elizabeth asked, raising an eyebrow.

When the three sisters all shook their heads, Elizabeth said again, "Come with me."

They walked with her through the quiet streets of Beckham until they reached Elizabeth's house on Rock Creek Road.

They stepped across the threshold, and Ana felt as if there was safety closing around her.

Elizabeth led them to the back of the house, to the last door on the left. She moved behind the desk in the room, and they took seats on the sofa that faced the desk.

The room was cluttered but it was an organized clutter. It was obviously a room that was used for work, and slightly messy out of necessity. Ana sat between her sisters, holding their hands and watching Elizabeth, wondering exactly what she had in mind for them.

Elizabeth smiled. "I don't think any of you know what I do for a living."

The three sisters looked at one another, shaking their heads in unison. "No, we don't," Rosie said softly.

"I'm a matchmaker. I send women west to marry men who are looking for wives."

Ana's eyes narrowed as she realized what Elizabeth was thinking. "You want us to become mail-order brides."

"Only if that's what you want," Elizabeth said softly.

"We have to be together," Ana said. "We're stronger together than apart."

"I have three letters from men who all live in the same town and decided to write me together. Would you be willing to read them and then make your decision?"

Ana looked at her sisters, who both nodded. "All right. We can do that."

Elizabeth handed the sisters three letters. They each took one and read it carefully. "I have yours," Rosie said to Izzy.

"I think I have yours," Izzy replied.

Ana read her letter, and she knew she had the letter she was supposed to have. Her heart reached out to the man who sent it across the miles, and she knew he was meant for her.

Dear Prospective Companion,

My name is Dr. William Mercer, and within the quiet solitude of this early morning, I am reaching out with a hope that this letter will find itself with a woman who is interested in changing her life as well as my own.

Hope Springs, nestled amidst the towering peaks and verdant valleys of the great state of Colorado, is a community built on the silver that is found in the mines near here. In my role as the town's physician, I have had the privilege of witnessing the strength and tenderness of the human spirit, of being there in moments of joy and sorrow. It is a life rich in purpose, but I find myself alone in a world where people are meant to pair off, two by two.

It is with a gentle, yet earnest heart that I seek a companion to share in the beauty and trials of this life. I long for someone with whom to share the quiet moments, the simple joys that fill the days—be it a walk through the aspens or the comforting silence of a snow-covered morning. A woman whose presence would transform the mere walls of a house into a home, filled with laughter, warmth, and the soft glow of shared dreams.

I envision a partner who cherishes kindness, values empathy, and holds a deep appreciation for both the vulnerability and strength found in caring for others. Life here is a tapestry of breathtaking beauty and stark challenges, and I seek one who is ready to stand by my side to share a future that honors both our individual journeys and our path forward.

In you, I hope to find not only a wife but a true partner in every sense of the word—a confidante, a source of mutual inspiration, and a co-custodian of the compassionate values that guide my practice and my life. Together, I believe we can build a life marked by love, understanding, and a deep commitment to the well-being of each other and those around us.

If these words speak to your heart, if you too dream of a life built upon the foundations of love, respect, and shared purpose, then I eagerly await your reply. Let us take the first tentative steps toward a future where, side by side, we may discover the depth of connection and the boundless possibilities that await us.

With hopeful anticipation and a heart open to the promise of tomorrow,

Dr. William Mercer

Hope Springs, Colorado

After reading the letter once more, Ana hugged it to her chest. "I found the letter that was meant for me."

"I won't mince words," Elizabeth said. "The journey itself isn't difficult, as train tracks are stretching across our great nation, but life in the West isn't as easy as it is here."

"We understand," Rosie said softly. "But the gentleman who wrote this letter is the man I intend to spend my life with."

Izzy nodded. "I agree. We want to go."

"Such journeys are not without peril," Elizabeth continued. "The West is a land of extremes—of fierce beauty and fierce challenges. But it would be a place away from your father, and you would be safe there."

Their collective breaths seemed to hold, suspended in the space between longing and fear. The prospect of leaving everything they knew loomed large, yet the more they considered Elizabeth's proposition, the more the tendrils of possibility wound through their doubts.

"I'm sure this is what we're meant to do," Ana said. "Mother taught us to have faith. And it's faith we need now. Faith that this path may lead us to a place where we're not watching over our shoulders in fear."

Izzy lifted her chin, eyes alight with a tempered spark. "We're going West," she affirmed.

"West," Rosie agreed.

"I'll wire the three gentlemen and ask them to fetch you from the train station in Hope Springs. I think we need to get the three of you on the next train out of town."

Ana nodded. "We have no wedding dresses."

"The men won't mind. They need wives, and they don't expect them to come with wedding dresses. These gentlemen all have what they need, and they'll be able to provide what you need as well."

Elizabeth walked to the closed door of her office, and called out, "Bernard!"

A tall man with blond hair was there a moment later. "What is it?" he asked, nodding politely to the three sisters.

"These three sisters need to leave town right away. I'm sending them to the three men in Colorado whose letters we received a few weeks ago. I'll need you to drive them to the station and stay with them until they are safely on the train."

Bernard nodded. "Yes, of course."

Elizabeth smiled. "Misses Winslow, this is my husband, Bernard."

"It's nice to meet you," Ana said, her sisters nodding their agreement.

Bernard looked at the carpet bag they carried with them. "Is that all you have?" he asked.

Rosie nodded. "Yes, it's all we have between us."

"We know it's not much," Izzy added.

Bernard nodded. "I'll have the buggy ready in fifteen minutes, and we'll go straight to the train station."

Ana felt her heart thundering in her chest as she nodded. "We're ready when you are."

They said their goodbyes to Elizabeth, thanking her for her help. "We'll forever be in your debt," Rosie whispered as she clutched Elizabeth's hands. "Thank you."

Once they were all in the buggy on the way to the train station, it hit Ana how quickly their lives were changing. "Never again will we be able to walk down by the creek and dip our feet into its cool depths."

"Never again will we have to be afraid to walk downstairs in the morning," Izzy said, shaking her head.

Rosie took each of their hands in her own. "But we'll always be together. We can't ask for more than that."

As they reached the train station, they all piled out of the buggy while Bernard bought their tickets. Then he waited with them until the train came fifteen minutes later. "Be safe," he whispered as he escorted them to the conductor. "But more importantly, be happy."

As they got onto the train and Rosie and Izzy sat together, Ana sat down opposite them. None of them had ever been on a train, and it felt strange to watch Beckham disappear out the window, but it was good. They were free.

Chapter Two

The shrill whistle of the locomotive pierced the mountain air as they stopped in Hope Springs. Anabelle's pulse raced as she stepped onto the wooden platform, her boots clacking against the planks. The scent of coal smoke and pine lingered, a harsh yet comforting reminder of the new world she was about to embrace. Her sisters stepped off beside her, and she reached out for Izzy's hand, knowing Izzy and Rosie were already clutching each other.

Her eyes roved over the crowd. Most were unfamiliar, etched with the lines of lives she had yet to know or understand. But then she saw him—a man carrying a little black bag that screamed doctor to her. She felt her heart skip a beat as their eyes met.

He did not smile nor wave. His gaze simply held hers. She felt as if he was giving her an unspoken promise to make the next portion of her life better than the first.

The platform around them thrummed with life, yet at that moment, the clamor receded into a distant murmur. For Ana, this meeting was the first breath above water—a glimmer of something resembling hope amid relentless uncertainty.

Dr. Mercer's hand reached out to her. As she placed her palm in his, the solid weight of his grasp spoke of strength.

"Dr. Mercer," Ana began, her voice a soft note against the whispering winds, "these are my sisters, Izzy and Rosie." She gestured to the two figures standing a respectful distance away. "Each is set to marry here in Hope Springs," she continued.

Ana stepped forward, her hand still clasped in Dr. Mercer's. Thoughts of her sisters faded as she left the platform with her future husband. She looked all around her at the small, quiet town. Children were playing in the streets and dust-covered miners strode toward their homes.

They hadn't walked far when they reached the church. Its wooden doors stood open, inviting the couple inside, where the air was still and silent. Stained glass filtered the sunlight into colors that danced upon the aisle where futures were forged.

"Miss Winslow," the preacher's voice was gentle, yet it held the weight of the moment, "are you prepared to enter into this holy union?"

Her heart caught. The question seemed to fill every corner of the church. Glancing toward the doorway, she thought of her sisters, each stepping onto their own paths, away from her side. They had been together every day of their lives, and now, even though they'd be in the same community, they would no longer share a room and always be together.

"Yes," she whispered, the word a fluttering bird in the vast sky of the church. It was an affirmation of survival, of the need to belong somewhere, with someone, even if it was a stranger whose kindness was the only thing she could yet call familiar.

Dr. Mercer's thumb brushed her knuckles—a silent vow beyond the words they exchanged. They turned to face each other, his kind eyes searching hers.

"Then by the power vested in me," the preacher intoned, his voice rising with conviction, "I now pronounce you husband and wife."

As the phrase settled over them, Ana felt frightened for a moment. She was bound now to this man, this town, to a life she had yet to discover. There was no time for farewells to her sisters or the life she once knew. She was his now, and he was hers.

They emerged from the church, the door closing behind them with a soft click, sealing the covenant just made. Ana looked up at the Rockies. In the quiet, amongst the fading day, she sensed the stirrings of hope. Hope that he would love her. Hope that he was kind. Hope that he wasn't anything like her father.

Dr. Mercer led Ana away from the church. There was a row of cottages that seemed to line the street.

"Here we are," he said, stopping before a house. Ana's breath caught at the sight, the charm of the home tugging at a place deep within her—a place she hadn't realized was hollow until now.

As far as she remembered, she'd only been in two homes in her entire life. The one where she grew up as well as Elizabeth Tandy's mansion. And now, she would step into the home she would share with her husband and raise a family in.

He turned the key in the lock and opened the door wide, his hand sweeping in a gentle arc, inviting her into their life together.

Ana crossed the threshold, her gaze sweeping across the parlor. The furnishings all looked comfortable, and she could see herself sitting in front of the fire. A quilt lay draped over a rocking chair, patches of faded fabric speaking of hands that had once worked the needle with care—hands that were no longer there.

"Welcome home, Anabelle," he said.

"Thank you," she replied. "Most people call me Ana."

She turned from the fire. Her fingers trailed along the back of the settee, the fabric worn smooth by time and touch.

"May I?" She gestured to the wooden seat by the hearth, seeking permission in this space that was theirs—but still his.

"Of course," Dr. Mercer assured her. "Everything here is as much yours as it is mine."

Settling into the chair, Ana allowed herself a moment to simply be—to listen to the crackle of the fire, to feel the cushion yield beneath her, to know that this, too, was life. Not a life she had envisioned, but one that held great potential.

"I thought we could eat at the restaurant in town this evening," he said. "I need to stop by the infirmary for a few minutes, and I don't want you to feel like you have to cook after your long journey, and I don't cook for people." He still held his doctor's bag, and she couldn't help but wonder if he'd take it to bed with him.

"You can cook but you don't cook for people?" she asked.

He shook his head. "Trust me. No one wants to eat anything I've made myself. I've grown a tolerance for my own cooking over the years."

Ana laughed softly. "My mother was an excellent cook, and she taught my sisters and me well."

"I'm glad to hear it. I'm looking forward to having meals waiting for me when I come home."

They stepped outside, and Dr. Mercer—William, she reminded herself—took Ana's hand, guiding her through the pathways of Hope Springs. The town seemed quite busy to her, with people rushing everywhere.

"Evening, Doc!" a burly man called out.

"Good evening, Tom," Dr. Mercer replied with a nod. "Meet my wife, Ana."

As she greeted the miners, rough hands shook hers with unexpected gentleness.

Ana's heart thrummed with a poignant ache as she witnessed the camaraderie among them—their laughter echoing off the wooden facades of buildings. A sense of loss gripped her, mourning the absence of her own kin, yet she found solace in the companionship offered by these strangers.

And her sisters would be close by when she found them. They would all live here, in this quaint little town, and they would be able to see each other. Often, she hoped.

A sharp voice cut through the hum of the evening. A man stood on the corner, his figure imposing against the backdrop of the general store.

"Mercer, we need to discuss this now. Progress doesn't wait for the indecisive," he said.

Dr. Mercer halted, releasing Ana's hand. She hovered nearby, feeling the shift in the air as two worlds collided.

"John, our people aren't pawns in your game of expansion," Dr. Mercer stated firmly.

"Your people? A doctor should know better than to stand in the way of growth," Thompson retorted.

Ana watched from across the street where the doctor left her. Though snippets of their debate reached her ears, the reason behind their argument remained a mystery to her. Yet, the implications were clear. The town was divided about something.

Finally, the man called John left, and Ana followed Dr. Mercer down the dirt road that wound through Hope Springs, her boots stirring small clouds of dust with each step. His voice was soft yet fervent as he spoke, the words falling like gentle rain on her upturned face.

"Hope Springs was born from these mountains," he said, gesturing toward the Rockies. "The mines have been the lifeblood of this town since its founding. They're more than just pits in the earth."

He shook his head. "Without the mines, we lose not only our economic stability but also our identity," he continued, locking eyes with hers. "These people, their sweat and toil, are what make us who we are. We can't let that slip away."

They entered the modest infirmary, where the scent of antiseptic mingled with the warmth of hearth fires. The waiting room held miners with calloused hands and lined faces, their expressions a blend of pain and stoicism. As Dr. Mercer approached, their eyes lit up with a reverence that spoke volumes.

"Doc, you're a sight for sore eyes," one grizzled man said, his tone rich with respect.

"Let's take a look at those eyes, then," Dr. Mercer replied, a smile crinkling the corners of his gaze.

Ana watched as he moved among them, his hands sure and gentle, his manner imbuing calm. The townspeople leaned into his touch, trust emanating from every pore. Each bandage applied, each reassuring word offered, was a stitch in the tapestry of communal life, binding them closer with threads of care.

In that quiet place, surrounded by the soft shuffle of feet and the muted clink of medical instruments, Ana's heart swelled. He was a compassionate man.

As she observed him, the melancholy that had haunted her since her arrival seemed to disappear, replaced by a growing sense of purpose. She was no longer an outsider looking in, but the doctor's partner.

After a quick supper, he took her to a spot where she could see the mountains and the sun setting behind them.

"Beautiful, isn't it?" Dr. Mercer murmured.

She nodded, her eyes tracing the rugged line of the Rockies, etched stark against the sky now ablaze with the hues of sunset. Ana breathed in deeply, the crisp air filling her lungs, laced with the scent of pine and the unseen promise of snow.

A cool breeze danced around them, lifting strands of her fiery red hair, playing with them like ribbons in the wind.

"Feels like the world is holding its breath," she said, her words barely louder than the rustle of leaves.

Dr. Mercer's hand found hers, a solid presence in the fading light. "And we're here to breathe with it," he replied, his thumb caressing the back of her hand in silent understanding.

Ana looked at their intertwined fingers, a tangible symbol of their newfound companionship. The loss of her mother, the ache of leaving everything known behind—all but her sisters.

"Ready to go back?" Dr. Mercer asked after a time, his question hanging between them like a gentle invitation.

"Yes," Ana affirmed, her voice steady, a testament to her resolve. She allowed herself one last lingering glance at the town below.

As they walked back toward the home she would share with him, Ana couldn't help but wonder if she and her sisters had made the right choice. They'd crossed the country to marry strangers, knowing they would at least live close enough they could take refuge with one another if something happened. And now, here they were, separated as soon as they reached town.

She hoped she would see her sisters soon, and they would be able to still see one another daily.

As she glanced at the doctor, she couldn't help but wonder what the night had in store for her. Would he expect her to be willing to make love that night? Or would he agree to put things off?

Either way, she knew she was in a better place than she had been in Massachusetts. She felt no fear when she was with the doctor. Thank heavens, he seemed to be as different from her father as day and night.

Chapter Three

Ana's fingers trembled slightly as she unpacked the small satchel that all of her belongings were in. She lifted out her garments, each piece folded with care, and placed them one by one into the empty dresser that stood against the wall. She only had two dresses so there wasn't much to put away. She would have to ask the doctor for money to buy fabric to make more, and she prayed it wouldn't upset him. If it did, she and her sisters still had the money their mother had given them for train fare, but she liked the idea of holding that in reserve, just in case something happened.

Ana paused. She took in the modest room with its sparse furnishings and the quilted bedspread. The weight of her past, the loss of her mother, and the ache of separation from her sisters pressed on her chest. For the first time in a long while, she felt the stirrings of peace.

She stepped lightly down the narrow hallway, drawn by the low glow beneath the study door. Dr. Mercer sat there, his figure bent over piles of medical records and journals. His pen moved with steady purpose, and she sensed the silent strength that drove him to continue working for the sake of Hope Springs' residents.

"Mind if I join you?" Her voice was soft.

He looked up, his eyes holding the warmth of a hearth fire. "Please," he said, motioning to the chair beside him.

She settled into the seat, folding her hands in her lap as she observed him return to his work. She needed to get to know him better. What had made him want to be a doctor? What made him work so hard for his patients?

He picked up one of the instruments and showed it to her. "This is a stethoscope," he explained, his voice a calm current in the stillness. "It lets us hear the sounds of the heart and lungs."

He slowly went through each of his instruments and let her touch them. Each item he passed into her care carried its own tale of healing, of hope wrestled from the clutches of illness.

"I'll need you to keep the instruments clean for me, and at times act as my nurse," he said.

"Thank you," Anabelle murmured, "for trusting me with this." She'd always hated that she hadn't been allowed to have a formal education, and she loved that he was teaching her now. Acting as a nurse seemed to be a way she could pay him back for his generosity in helping her escape from her father's clasp.

When he felt she'd learned enough, the two of them made their way to the modest bedroom they now shared. They lay down, side by side.

It felt strange to Ana to be in a bed with anyone but her sisters, but she knew it was her role to share a bed with him, even if she was frightened. She could already see he was a good man, which helped her not worry quite so much.

Sleep beckoned, but Ana lingered in wakefulness, savoring the solace found in her companion's nearness. In the hush of night, amid the ghosts of a day's end, she allowed herself a fragile hope. Perhaps this was the place where she and her sisters would find true joy. Even if they didn't, they were at least beyond the reach of their father and his fists.

"William," she whispered, her voice barely rising above the stillness. His name felt new on her lips.

Dr. Mercer turned to her, his eyes questioning. "Yes, Ana?"

She swallowed hard, her hands clasped together in her lap as if they could steady the fluttering within. "Would it be all right if we—if we waited? To—to consummate our marriage?" The words tumbled out, and she blushed when she heard her voice speak them aloud.

A softness entered his gaze, the edges of his eyes crinkling with empathy. "Of course," he replied, his voice a balm to her racing thoughts. "I never imagined that I would have a wedding night with a woman I'd just met."

Anabelle nodded. "It's very strange," she began again, her voice steadier now, "My sisters— we're triplets. Izzy, Rosie, and I. We've never spent a night apart, always sharing whispers until sleep took us." Her eyes misted over, the memory a stark contrast to the solitude of this new room. "It feels strange, being without them, like a piece of my soul is missing."

William reached out, his hand covering hers.

William's gaze held her own, steady and certain. "We'll find your sisters," he said, his voice low but resolute in the dim light. "I know the men they were promised to. Good, honest men. We're all friends and agreed to send off for mail-order brides together. I'm pleased we all married sisters because that will only strengthen our bond with one another."

"Thank you," she whispered, the weight of loneliness beginning to lift from her shoulders. The promise of reuniting with Izzy and Rosie was one she'd needed to hear.

She nestled deeper into the quilts that adorned their shared bed, drawing comfort from their warmth. Her eyelids grew heavy, the events of the day—the vows exchanged, the journey made—catching up to her at last. She turned slightly, feeling William's presence beside her, a solid, reassuring constant in this new world.

As sleep beckoned, her mind wandered through the streets of Hope Springs, imagining her sisters nearby, laughter mingling with the crisp mountain air. A smile graced her lips as she succumbed to dreams. Here she and her sisters would still be part of one another's lives, and they would be happy.

THE SUN WASN'T UP YET when Ana climbed from the warmth of her bed. Her feet touched the cold wooden floor, and she suppressed a shiver as she wrapped her shawl tighter around her slender shoulders. She moved through the quiet rooms, her heart heavy with thoughts of days long past.

The quiet in this house should have felt the same as the constant quiet in the house where she'd grown up. But there, she'd had her sisters whispering with her, and here...she was alone. But there was no waiting for the yells that would punctuate her father's moods. Instead, she could simply move about without fear. Well, she could move about. The fear would eventually leave her. She hoped.

She walked into the kitchen and looked through the cabinets, familiarizing herself with how it was set up. With practiced motions, she stoked the fire in the stove and set a skillet atop it. Eggs lay on the counter, next to a loaf of bread. She cracked them one by one into the sizzling pan.

William, roused by the sounds and smells of breakfast, joined her in the kitchen. His hair was tousled from sleep, his eyes soft with the vulnerability that morning often brings. "Smells delightful," he commented, a gentle smile gracing his lips as he watched her flip the eggs with a deft flick of her wrist.

"Thank you," Ana replied. A small pride fluttered in her chest. She was not used to receiving compliments, and it made her feel like she could stand a little taller.

"Is it your habit to attend church on Sundays?" William asked casually, leaning against the doorframe, his gaze lingering on her face, searching for glimpses into her upbringing.

Ana paused, the spatula hovering above the pan. The question stirred memories of mornings arrayed in scratchy collars and tight braids, mother's whispered prayers swallowed by father's stern decree. "We used to," she said softly, placing the eggs onto plates. "But not for many years."

Ana settled into the chair across from William, her fingers tracing the wood grain of the table as she gathered her thoughts. "When I was little," she began, her voice a mere whisper against the hushed stillness of the room, "we would go to church every Sunday, and Mother would dress us in matching dresses. She loved that we were triplets and wanted us to always look alike." She glanced up at him, her eyes reflecting a pool of memories. "But that all changed when I turned five."

William's furrowed brow betrayed his surprise. He set his fork down gently, a silent invitation for her to continue.

"Father decided it was best if we stayed away from...from everything outside our home," Ana said, a shadow passing over her features. "We never saw the inside of a schoolhouse. Mother taught us while Father worked. He didn't want us knowing how to read and write, but Mother said we would be pleased that we could."

"Isolated," he murmured.

"Sometimes," she confessed, "we would find moments of freedom." A wistful smile curled the edges of her lips. "While father worked the fields, my sisters and I would slip through the creaky back gate and dance beneath the sky, pretending we were part of a world that didn't know our names." She shook her head. "Two years ago, we made it into town. We talked to everyone we saw and had a wonderful time. Until Father found us." She didn't have to add that being found was not a good thing for any of them.

William watched her, a mingling of admiration and concern etched into the lines of his face. He wanted more details, but he wasn't sure it would be right to ask. Instead, he'd let her open up about her past in her own time.

"Your cooking," he said, breaking the silence, "it's quite remarkable, Ana."

She offered a small smile, tucking a stray lock of fiery hair behind her ear. His compliment warmed her, an ember of pride glowing within.

"Thank you," she replied.

He watched her for a moment, then cleared his throat gently. "I usually attend church on Sunday mornings," William ventured, his gaze steady. "Would you... would you care to join me today?"

"I would like that very much," Ana answered, her voice barely above a whisper. She liked the idea of going to church again, as she had when she was small.

As she gazed at William, a torrent of memories surged forth. Church had been a place of shared whispers and laughter with Izzy and Rosie. It had been a haven until it wasn't. Now, the anticipation of seeing her sisters there, amidst the flock of faithful, electrified her spirit.

"Then we shall go after breakfast," he said, a gentle nod sealing the plan.

Ana turned away, hiding the tremor of excitement that coursed through her. Oh, how she hoped her sisters would be there. It was strange not knowing where they were. She couldn't remember a time in her life when she'd been unaware of her sisters' location.

Ana and William walked side by side to the church. The town was small, and William seemed to walk everywhere he went. Surely, he had a buggy for out of town calls though.

The wooden doors of the church loomed ahead, familiar in their imposing stature. It was here they had spoken vows, words that still echoed in her mind like a lingering promise. She glanced at William, his profile etched with the same resolve she found in his voice every time he spoke of healing others.

"Good morning, Dr. Mercer," called a soft voice as they stepped into the cool sanctuary of the church. Gertrude Hannigan stood near the entrance, the pastor's young wife, cradling her infant close to her chest. The baby cooed, a sound pure and untouched by the world's harsh whispers.

"Ana, this is Gertrude Hannigan," William introduced with a slight tilt of his head. "She's the pastor's wife."

"Mrs. Hannigan," Ana greeted. Gertrude offered a smile warm enough to ease the tightness in Ana's chest, the baby's fingers curling around her mother's thumb.

"Welcome to our community," Gertrude said, shifting the baby to one arm. "Let me introduce you to some of the other ladies."

Ana nodded, following Gertrude's lead as they weaved through clusters of townspeople. Names and faces blurred together, each introduction adding a bit more confusion to Ana's mind. The women's voices were a low hum, punctuated by the occasional high-pitched laugh that seemed almost foreign to Ana's ears. Being in a crowd like this after so many years of solitude...it was overwhelming.

Izzy and Rosie, her sisters, stood together at the back of the church. Their presence was a beacon, and it was calling her to them. Ana's heart lurched, her feet moving before her mind could catch up.

"Excuse me," she murmured, though it was unlikely Gertrude heard her over the chatter. Ana navigated through the sea of Sunday bests, the rustle of petticoats whispering secrets.

Her sisters turned as she approached, their faces lighting up with recognition and a shared joy that no distance or time could diminish. She spread her arms wide, and the three of them embraced. All at once she was home. It was strange that home to her wasn't a place. It was her sisters.

Ana's fingers intertwined with those of her sisters. Rosie's eyes shimmered with the same strength that had always defined her, and Izzy's gentle smile offered solace in its familiarity.

"Charles Jordan," Rosie whispered, her voice tinged with a mixture of pride and something more guarded, "He has a kind heart." The name was etched into Ana's mind, alongside the image of her sister, now intertwined with another's fate.

Izzy spoke next, her words soft as the drape of lace over a Sunday dress, "And I am by Albert Thoreau's side. He's a good man. And extremely smart. I'm fortunate to be his wife."

The church bell tolled, a somber reminder that life's dance continued beyond the sanctuary of sisterhood. Ana released her hold, her touch lingering like the last rays of twilight against the horizon.

"Come, let us find our seats," she murmured, turning toward the gathering congregation, her skirts whispering secrets into the hush of the sanctuary.

With each step, Ana felt the weight of her new reality settle upon her shoulders like a shawl woven from the threads of duty and desire. She slid into the pew beside William. It was strange to know her sisters were in the building, but her place was here with her new husband.

Her gaze drifted over her shoulder, seeking the familiar sights of her sisters among the flock. She knew she had to find them again after the service was over.

As the preacher's voice rose and fell about loving thy neighbor, Ana's thoughts danced between the words spoken and those held close to her heart. Each glance backward, a lifeline cast into the past, each hymn sung, a step toward the morrow.

The church doors swung open. Ana stepped into the light, William's hand a reassuring weight upon her back as they descended the wooden steps together. The world outside shimmered with the promise of Sunday repose, and there, waiting at the foot of the church, were Rosie and Charles, Izzy and Albert.

"Shall we?" Charles gestured toward the direction of the local eatery, his voice carrying the lilting cadence of camaraderie.

Ana's lips curved up ever so slightly, a bloom of pleasure at the sight of the men, her William included, falling into easy conversation as they ambled down the road. The gravel crunched beneath their boots, a chorus to the harmony that seemed to unfurl between them.

Eyes bright, Ana watched William exchange words with Albert, who nodded thoughtfully, his face marked by the stern lines of responsibility. Beside them, Charles's laughter rang clear, the sound like water over pebbles, smoothing out the edges of the day.

They arrived at the modest establishment, the same place where Ana had eaten with William the night before. Inside, the scent of fresh bread and roasted meat filled the air, an invisible thread weaving through the hearts of all who entered.

As they settled around a worn oak table, the sisters exchanged glances, a silent language honed by years of whispered confidences. It was not lost on them—the way the townsfolk greeted their husbands with nods of respect, the way the waitress deferred to William's selections, the quiet authority that seemed to emanate from each man.

Ana felt the subtle shift in the room, the unspoken recognition of their husbands' places within Hope Springs. Dr. Mercer, the healer, Charles Jordan, the mayor with hands that shaped the laws of the town, and Albert Thoreau, a wealthy businessman who had found his start in the silver mines surrounding the town.

As they ate, the men carried on an animated conversation, while Ana and her sisters listened, exchanging glances that said as much as the men said aloud.

It was hard to say goodbye to her sisters after they left the restaurant. But Ana had made a promise to meet them at the general store at one in the afternoon the following day. They all needed church dresses, as they had not had anything new in years. They would need to buy fabric, and she hoped there would be time for the three of them to sew together.

Ana walked beside William toward their home. "Thank you for the time with my sisters," Ana said softly.

William smiled. "I'm glad they can continue to be a part of your life here."

As they turned down Main Street, a figure approached—a man who walked with pride, his sharp eyes scanning the horizon like a hawk. It was John Thompson, and he looked angry.

"Ana, would you mind waiting for me across the street by the general store?" William's voice was calm, but the tension in his jaw betrayed an underlying urgency.

Without question or hesitation, she nodded, crossing to where he pointed, her heart fluttering with unease. The distance muffled their words, but not the gravity of their exchange. William's stance was firm, his hand gesturing with restrained emphasis. John's smile never reached his eyes as he leaned in, a whisper of aggression in his poise.

When at last William crossed back to her, his face was a mask of composure. "Who was that?" Ana's voice barely rose above a whisper, her gaze searching his for clues.

"Nobody of concern, Ana." His answer was a gentle brush-off, meant to shield her from the storm brewing beneath the surface. But the weight of his dismissal hung heavy in the air, a specter of things unspoken.

Ana stole glances at William, feeling the resonance of his concealed worries. She yearned to share his burden, to understand the forces that drove him, yet she sensed the protective barriers he erected were not solely for her sake, but for the community he served.

As they neared the home they now shared, the somber reality settled upon Ana's shoulders—a life intertwined with another's, filled with companionship and loss, secrets and silences.

Chapter Four

Ana sat across from William at breakfast on Monday morning. "William," she began, "I've been thinking...I would like to make myself a new dress for church." She was almost afraid to ask, thinking about the way her father had beaten her mother when she'd asked for money to buy fabric for dresses for her and her sisters.

William looked up from his plate. A slow smile spread across his face, the kind that instantly put Ana's worries to rest. "That sounds like a splendid idea, Ana," he said, nodding. His hand reached for the leather pouch by his side and he counted out several coins, laying them before her with care. "This should cover your needs for the household, and a little something extra for your dress."

"Thank you, William. That's more than generous." She tucked the coins into her apron pocket, feeling the weight of them against her thigh.

"Later today, after lunchtime, I shall meet my sisters at the general store." Her gaze met his. "We wish to choose the fabric together."

"Of course," he replied, his voice steady. There was no hesitation, only the clear understanding of family bonds. "I know you're all close. Enjoy your time with them."

Ana nodded, a small smile creasing her lips as she imagined the colorful bolts of fabric. She'd never been able to come and go as she pleased, but William seemed to think allowing her to spend time out of the house was a normal thing to do. She wasn't sure what to do with all the freedom he offered.

William closed the discussion on the household budget with a nod, his hand lingering on the edge of the table as he stood. "I'll be back for lunch," he said, glancing toward the kitchen. The scent of fresh bread still hung in the air—a comforting reminder of their morning meal shared. "If you're pressed for time, Ana, do not fret. A sandwich will suffice."

Ana watched him don his coat, the lines of concern etched lightly upon his brow easing with her assurance. "You needn't worry about going hungry," she replied. "Three meals a day is what I promised, and three meals a day you shall have."

He paused at the door, a smile tugging at the corner of his mouth, a silent acknowledgment of her steadfast resolve. But Ana's thoughts were already drifting to the dress. Never had she been allowed to choose fabric and make a dress for herself. Her father had done all the shopping, and her mother would make the most of whatever he'd brought home for them.

"Today, though," she continued, "the new dress takes precedence. There's no mending more pressing than preparing to look decent for Sunday's sermon."

As the door clicked shut behind him, Ana let out a breath she hadn't realized she'd been holding. Alone again, the silence settled around her. She turned back to the window, the glass cool beneath her fingertips, and gazed out at the world awakening beyond.

She had always had her sisters beside her. It was odd to be truly alone, and she wished she could have them with her all the time. She knew it would be good to learn to be alone, but she wasn't certain she was ready.

Memories of a life once filled with the constant hum of her sisters' voices tugged at the edges of her mind—three lives intertwined, now unraveled into separate threads. And as she prepared for William's return, she clung to the thought of that reunion. They'd seen one another briefly the day before, but none of them had been able to truly share her thoughts with the others. She needed to know her sisters were safe. She needed them to know she was safe.

ANA HURRIED THROUGH the streets of Hope Springs, along the dirt road that meandered like a dried-up riverbed. She held William's money close—a sum for her own whims and the needs of their household—and with it, a sense of autonomy that both thrilled and unnerved her.

The general store was just ahead, and there, beneath the awning, Isabelle and Rosabelle waited.

"Finally," Izzy said as Ana approached.

"Thought you'd never come," Rosie added.

They entered the store together, making a beeline for the table piled high with fabric. There were so many colors and textures begging to be touched and transformed.

"Something modest, yet fetching," Ana mused aloud, fingers tracing over calico and gingham. She felt that she should get the same fabric as her sisters, as they'd always dressed alike, but they were no longer three parts of one whole. They were each married and must show their individual tastes.

"I like this one," Izzy said, her hand resting on a pattern of delicate ivy on a field of cream.

"Or this." Rosie held up an identical design, but where Isabelle's choice was soft and gentle, hers was a dusky rose, grounded and unassuming.

"William said I could choose." Ana's voice held a note of wonder, though no one knew better than her sisters the weight of the word 'could'.

"Then we shall all have the same," Rosie declared with a nod that settled the matter. "In different hues, reflecting each of us."

"Reflections of the same soul," Izzy whispered, and they cut three lengths from similar bolts—cream for Izzy, rose for Rosie, and a vibrant green for Ana.

Ana smiled. "Now we'll have the same pattern, but won't look like we're trying to look exactly alike."

With their purchases bundled in their arms, they stepped back outside. For now, they were together again, and soon, they would be able to share secrets. All felt right with the world again.

"I need to stop at the butcher to get meat for supper. Do you mind?" Ana asked her sisters.

When Izzy and Rosie both shook their heads, she hurried into the butcher shop. After a brief exchange of pleasantries, she pointed to a cut of meat. It was practical, enough for William and her both. Tonight, she would cook supper in her new home, a ritual of domesticity that was both foreign and familiar.

"Will you show us where you live now?" Izzy asked as they exited the store, her voice soft as the cream fabric tucked under her arm.

"Of course," Ana replied, leading the way. Her sisters trailed behind her. They didn't speak until they reached her home, and Ana unlocked the door to lead her sisters inside.

"Let's bake cookies," Rosie suggested. "Tea would be lovely."

Ana looked at her sisters, stunned for a moment. "I guess we're allowed to cook and bake whatever we want now, aren't we?"

Izzy nodded. "I made a meal for supper last night, and it was so odd that I could choose whatever I wanted and not worry about Father's wrath. It's a whole new world, feeling this much freedom. And yet..."

"It still feels like we should be watching over our shoulder for anger," Rosie finished for her sister. "I don't know how long it's going to take to really feel like we're free, but we're going to get there. All three of us."

Soon, the kitchen was filled with the aroma of sugar and butter, all the ingredients forming golden discs on the baking sheet. They sat around the table, sipping tea from mismatched cups, the rich taste mingling with the sweetness of the cookies.

"William is kind," Ana mused aloud, a confession wrapped in layers of uncertainty. "He speaks little, but his silences aren't cold."

"Albert is a good man filled with strong opinions," Izzy shared. "I'm afraid to disagree with him, even when I think he's wrong."

"Strength, Izzy," Ana whispered. "You'll find your place beside him."

Rosie's needle pierced the green fabric, her stitches perfect. "My husband, Charles, well, he's more like a puzzle. Each piece revealing itself slowly, methodically. He doesn't talk much, at least not to me."

Ana shook her head. "Did either of your husbands insist on a wedding night?"

Izzy nodded, blushing. "Albert did, but it wasn't bad. Just...different to have someone touching me that way."

Ana frowned. "William was fine with waiting. He doesn't show strong emotions about anything...except this one man he keeps arguing with. I have no idea what they argue about because he has me wait across the street."

"That's odd," Rosie said. "Do they argue often?"

"Twice now. Men are so confusing. I wish they could think like we do."

Izzy smiled. "I agree. But I wish Albert would share fewer opinions. I might be able to find out why William keeps arguing with someone if you'd like."

Ana shook her head. "No, William should be the one to tell me."

Ana threaded the needle with a deft hand, her movements sure and practiced. The sisters' conversation had dwindled to a comfortable silence, punctuated by the occasional clink of a teacup being set down.

"Father won't just let us vanish," Ana said suddenly, her voice softer than she intended. The thread trembled slightly in her grasp as she considered the possibility.

Izzy's laughter was a gentle chime. "He has his hands full with the farm. He won't leave it to find us."

"What if he hires someone?" Rosie asked. She shuddered delicately. "I have no idea what he would do about this kind of defiance."

Izzy frowned. "We're not girls anymore. We made our choices."

Ana's chest tightened at Izzy's dismissive tone. She knew Izzy was right, yet the fear of being chased by the past—a past that included a father who viewed his daughters as nothing more than punching bags—worried her more than she cared to admit.

"Father won't believe we made the right choices," Ana murmured, but her words were lost in the rustle of fabric.

The clock on the mantel struck, its chimes signaling the encroaching evening. Izzy stood first, smoothing the folds of her skirt. "Time to start supper. I need to get home," she said, her tone laced with a hint of reluctance.

Rosie also stood to gather her things, but her movements were slow, as if trying to stretch the minutes into hours. Rosie smiled at the other two. "Can we meet again around the same time tomorrow?" she asked, her hand resting briefly on Ana's shoulder.

"Please," Ana said softly.

Izzy nodded, and then she and Rosie left, leaving Ana to start supper for herself and William.

Ana watched through the window as her sisters' figures receded along the path, their heads close together in shared confidences. The house felt emptier, the air stiller. She returned to her unfinished dress, the fabric pooling in her lap.

With each stitch, memories wove themselves into the seams—their laughter echoing in the rafters of the barn, the warmth of bodies huddled together during cold nights, the collective strength they found in each other. Now, they had separate lives, and Ana said a quick prayer, thanking God for helping them all to be near one another.

Finally, Ana set aside her work. Her hands felt cold without the comfort of her sisters' presence. A deep longing settled in her heart, a yearning for the simplicity of yesterday, for the certainty of sisterhood.

Soon, the kitchen was warm, and the scent of roasting meat filled the small space as Ana moved with quiet efficiency. Potatoes sizzled softly in a pan, their edges crisping to a golden hue. She set the table, placing two plates with care.

When William stepped through the door, his presence seemed to chase away the shadows that had filled her with her sisters gone. He washed up at the basin, his hands deliberate and thorough, the physician in him never resting. They sat together, knee to knee, at the small table. Ana offered him a guarded smile, serving the food she had prepared.

"Smells wonderful," he said, his tone earnest, appreciative. They ate, the silence between them comfortable, companionable. It was a simple meal, but it tasted good, and she was pleased with it.

As the meal came to an end, William helped clear the table. The melancholy of solitude that had gripped Ana's heart eased under his quiet attentiveness. Together, they moved to the sitting area by the fire.

There, they talked of daily trivialities—the weather, the townsfolk, the minor ailments he'd treated.

And then, as if guided by an unseen hand, their conversation lulled, and they found themselves caught in a gaze that lingered too long. William reached out, his fingers brushing against hers, a touch that sparked a warmth that spread up her arm.

"Ana," he said, his voice barely above a whisper, "you've been a blessing I didn't know I was missing." His eyes searched hers.

Before she could think, before the doubts could resurface, their lips met. The kiss was gentle, a question asked and answered in the same breath. Ana's pulse quickened, her body awakening to a sensation she had never known she could command. Desire, bold and unbidden, coursed through her, leaving her breathless, astonished by the depth of her own longing.

They parted with cheeks flushed. William's hand lingered on her cheek, his thumb tracing the line of her jaw. Ana closed her eyes, leaning into the touch, memorizing the feel of him, the rightness of this moment.

"Thank you for supper," he said, his voice low, carrying a weight that held more than gratitude for the meal.

"Thank you for...everything," Ana replied, her words trailing off into the crackling of the fire. "I'm so thankful it doesn't bother you that I want to spend time with my sisters. Being triplets who weren't allowed to leave our home, we're used to always being together, and this is a big change for us."

"I would never dream of keeping you from your sisters." The look William gave her seemed filled with unspoken words, but she understood. How did you respond when someone tells you they've lived their whole life in isolation?

Much later, Ana put away the last of the dishes that she'd allowed to drip dry. William had excused himself, his footsteps fading toward the bedroom they now shared—a room that seemed both sanctuary and uncharted territory.

She paused at the doorway, hand resting against the frame. The memory of the kiss lingered on her lips. She had never imagined the waves of desire she felt with that kiss.

Ana watched William, the steady rise and fall of his chest, and felt a pull, a yearning to close the distance between them.

She approached the bed hesitantly, the wooden planks beneath her feet creaking in protest. Quickly changing into her nightdress, she slipped beneath the covers, the coolness of the sheets a stark contrast to the warmth radiating from William's body.

"Goodnight," she murmured, voice barely above a whisper.

"Goodnight, Ana." His reply held a note of something unspoken, a resonance that vibrated through the stillness.

Ana turned onto her side, facing away from him, staring into the darkness. Her mind replayed the evening in fragments—the laughter that danced around the supper table, the way William's eyes crinkled when he smiled, the feather-light touch of his lips.

After a long moment, she said, "I liked it when you kissed me. I hope we'll do that again."

He wasn't sure if he imagined her words, or if she'd really spoken them. Either way, he'd be kissing her again. And soon.

Chapter Five

na moved quietly around the infirmary, her hair pulled back in a practical braid, a stark contrast to the pallor of illness and injury surrounding her. She was a constant presence at her husband's side, assisting William as he made his rounds.

"Hand me the gauze, Ana," William's voice was soft but firm, breaking the hush that enveloped the space.

As William tended to a miner with a gash across his brow—a souvenir from a minor tunnel collapse—Ana's gaze lingered on the man's weathered face. She wondered about the life that had etched itself into his skin, about the dreams that lay beneath. The miner winced as the needle pierced flesh but gave a grateful nod toward Ana as she held his hand steady, her own fingers surprisingly calm.

"Almost done," William murmured, the furrow in his brow softening as the final stitch was placed. He looked up at Ana, his eyes reflecting a quiet appreciation. She offered him a small, reassuring smile in return, sensing the weight of his world on her shoulders—a weight she had willingly accepted.

Once the miner was bandaged and resting, Ana turned her attention to the ledger on William's desk. Her fingertips traced the lines of numbers and names, a record of the day's healing and heartache. Each entry was a life touched, and she handled the billing with a methodical precision that belied the emotion each figure represented. She mentally thanked her mother for all the arithmetic she and her sisters had been forced to do, thankful she could do the math necessary to keep her husband's books.

The scent of antiseptic and the muted sounds of recovery filled the air as Ana worked. A melancholy settled over her, born of the realization that for all the good they did here, there was always another name to add to the list, another wound to mend.

She closed the ledger, the soft thud echoing slightly in the stillness, and glanced at William. He was washing his hands, the water dripping in a slow, rhythmic patter against the metal basin.

"Thank you, Ana," he said.

"Of course, William," she replied.

Ana watched the clock's hands crawl toward noon, their relentless march a reminder of time slipping away. "I need to head home and get lunch ready for you."

William nodded. "I'll be home soon."

Once home, Ana made sandwiches out of the fresh bread she'd baked early that morning. She added bacon to each sandwich before placing them on the plates and carrying them to the table.

Just as she was pouring coffee for each of them, William walked in the door, looking tired. "I hope sandwiches are all right," she said.

William entered the kitchen. His smile was weary—a slight upturn of lips that didn't quite reach his eyes. "Yes, of course." He washed his hands, carefully scrubbing them all the way up to the elbow.

"Your lunch is ready," she said.

"Thank you, Ana." He moved to the table, sitting down and waiting for her to join him.

"Will you need me this afternoon?"

"No, I shouldn't think so." He took a bite of the sandwich. "Very good," he said. "You've been a great help this morning but go spend some time with your sisters. They'll be eager to see you."

"All right," Ana replied, nodding slowly. "If anything changes, I'll leave a note on the door for them."

"Unlikely," he assured her.

The rest of the meal passed in silence, and he ate quickly. "I need to get back to work."

"Have a good afternoon," she said.

The door closed behind him, and Ana was left alone in the silence that followed.

The room felt larger, emptier now that William had gone back to tend to his patients, the echoes of their morning together lingering like phantom caresses. She felt so alone with him gone. Thankfully her sisters would be there soon. Being alone was becoming a big part of her life, and she didn't like it one bit.

Ana moved with quiet purpose, setting a tray with freshly baked cookies and steeping tea. She laid out the delicate cups, their rims kissed by silver leaf.

Her sisters arrived just as she poured the tea. Their presence filled the space with a soft hum of conversation and the rustling of fabric as they settled around the table, each working diligently on their dresses, fingers dancing nimbly over seams and stitches.

Izzy, her hands cradling a teacup, broke the tender silence with a whisper that seemed both out of place and entirely fitting amidst the lace and linen. "I must confess," she began, her cheeks flushed, "Albert and I made love again last night... and something magical happened."

Ana's needle paused mid-air, her heart quickening at the revelation. Izzy's eyes sparkled with an inner light. "I can't quite describe it, but it was good—a feeling that words can't capture."

Izzy leaned forward, her voice a tender urging. "Don't wait any longer," she implored, "experience it for yourselves."

Ana folded her hands in her lap, the unfinished hem of her dress forgotten. Her thoughts drifted to William, to the tentative bond forming between them, a bridge constructed of shared silences and unspoken understandings. Could there be a magic waiting for them too, beyond the careful politeness and the chaste kisses?

Izzy's words resonated in the quiet of the room, a promise or perhaps a challenge. And Ana knew, with a clarity that pierced through the fog of her melancholy, that life—like the act of making love—was not meant to be observed from a distance, but to be lived, embraced, and savored in all its complexity.

Ana picked up a needle, and her fingers moved with the rhythm of practice as she stitched the delicate fabric of her dress, but her mind was elsewhere. Beneath her calm exterior, emotions swirled like leaves caught in an unseen whirlwind.

"William kissed me," she said suddenly. Her sisters paused, their own needles halting in mid-air.

"Really?" Rosie's question was a soft exhalation, a mixture of surprise and yearning.

"Last night," Ana continued, her gaze fixed on the tiny stitches. "We were talking, and our eyes met, and the next thing I knew we were kissing." She couldn't help the faint color that rose to her cheeks. The kiss had been brief, a fleeting connection.

"Was it..." Izzy hesitated, her eyes searching Ana's face for a hint of the magic she herself had experienced.

"Sweet," Ana replied, the corners of her mouth lifting ever so slightly. "Gentle."

Rosie resumed her sewing, her hands steady but she looked sad. "Charles has yet to kiss me," she admitted quietly. She didn't look up, afraid to see pity in her sisters' eyes. "I don't think he harbors any affection for me."

"That can't be true," Izzy offered, her tone encouraging.

"Very," Rosie agreed. "Charles is always there, a constant presence of quiet strength and unwavering respect. Perhaps love wasn't meant for me, but kindness is its own form of companionship, and for that, I'm grateful."

Ana reached across the table, placing her hand over Rosie's. The touch was silent solidarity, a shared understanding that even in the solitude of their arranged marriages, they were not alone. They had each other, and the hope of finding their own unique happiness.

Ana bid farewell to her sisters shortly before time to start supper. She turned to the stove. Carrots and potatoes sizzled gently in the skillet. As she cooked, she couldn't stop thinking about what Izzy had said about something magical happening when she made love with her husband. Could something magical happen for her and William as well?

Only now did it dawn on Ana—the glaring absence of passion in her own union. Her heart fluttered, a caged bird against the ribs of composure she had so carefully constructed. Rosie had mentioned she hadn't even been kissed. She was glad that she and William had done that once. Now they just needed to do it more.

After finishing the dishes, she found William in the sitting room. And though she was nervous about bringing up the topic of lovemaking with him, she was excited at the prospect of experiencing whatever Izzy had that she couldn't explain.

"William," she began, "I've been thinking..." She paused, the words lodged in her throat.

He looked up. "Yes, Ana?" he prompted.

"About us," she continued. "I believe...it may be time we considered becoming more intimate." Her cheeks flushed with the boldness of her declaration.

He regarded her, a furrow of surprise etching his brow, not expecting such blunt speak from his sweet wife. And yet, there was a warmth there, too.

"Are you certain, Ana?" His voice was soft, the question not one of reluctance, but of care.

Ana nodded. "I want to understand," she confessed, "to experience... whatever it was that made my sister's Izzy practically glow with satisfaction today."

"Very well," he replied, his hand reaching out to enclose hers.

The bedroom was dim. William stood watching as Ana's delicate fingers workedat the buttons of her blouse, an act so innocent and yet charged with the unspoken anticipation of what lay ahead.

"Ana," he began, his voice betraying a hint of the surprise that had settled in his chest. But he was a man of flesh and blood, with the same desires as any other. He stepped closer, his hands steady despite the adrenaline coursing through him.

Her breath caught, a soft gasp slipping from her lips as she gazed up at him.

He reached out, his touch tentative but sure, guiding her hands away from her task to rest within his own. Together, they finished the unbuttoning.

His fingers traced the lines of her collarbone, reverent and unhurried, mapping the geography of a land he vowed to cherish.

"Are you afraid?" he asked, his voice low.

"A little," Ana confessed.

"Then we'll take this slow," William assured her.

The bed creaked beneath their weight. Her heart thundered enough she was surprised he didn't hear it, as she allowed herself to be guided down onto the patchwork quilt.

His hands moved all over her, and she gasped at how good they felt against her bare flesh. And though the nervous flutter in her belly persisted, there was comfort in the careful way he honored her, his touch painting strokes of affection and reverence.

She found pleasure in the closeness, in the whisper of his breath against her skin, the strength of his arms holding her. It was a different joy than she'd imagined. It was somehow quieter. And while she enjoyed what they did together, a part of her seemed to be watching, searching for the rapture Izzy had spoken of with such fervor.

But as the night deepened, and they lay entwined, she realized that they had crossed a threshold together.

Their breaths mingled in the quiet space, his steady and hers still catching from time to time. Ana lay nestled in the crook of William's arm, her head resting against the solid rise and fall of his chest.

A soft sigh escaped her as she closed her eyes, the warmth of him seeping into her bones. She had been brave, stepping into the unknown with a man who was kind, whose eyes held stories she longed to hear. He had been so gentle, so patient, as if understanding the weight of her unspoken fears.

But in the depths of her being, a faint echo of longing stirred—a yearning for the elusive magic Izzy had found in the arms of her own husband.

She shifted in his embrace, and he tightened his hold.

As she drifted toward slumber, she found a flicker of hope. Perhaps in time, the pleasure her sister spoke of would find her too. For now, it was enough to feel the steady heartbeat of the man beside her, to know that they were creating a life together.

Ana's last conscious thought was thinking she must get more details from Izzy about when the magical thing had happened. Making love with William had been sweet, but not quite as magical as she'd hoped. But as she fell asleep, she decided she'd happily do it again, even with no magic. She could tell she'd pleased him, and that mattered.

Chapter Six

Ana stood at the edge of the mining camp, her gaze fixed on the jagged opening of the Hope Springs mine. The workers emerged into the light, faces smeared with soot. The aftermath of the latest accident lingered in the air like the dust that refused to settle—a cart derailed deep within the labyrinthine tunnels, trapping miners for hours.

From what Ana had observed the town was split. There were the men who had grown rich in the silver mines surrounding the town, and the current miners, who were lining the pockets of others. Everyone was either very rich or very poor, though she and William seemed to be right in the middle of them all.

She wrapped her shawl tighter around her shoulders. With each incident, the whispers grew louder, the suspicions more pointed. It was no longer a matter of simple misfortune. Something much more sinister was happening to their community.

"Ana," William said from behind her. He approached her from behind, his hand finding the small of her back.

"William," Ana replied, turning to face him. "There's talk among the men. They're saying these accidents are not just coincidence."

"We must tread carefully, Ana. Accusations demand evidence."

"Caution?" Ana's voice trembled slightly. "While we wait, men's lives hang by a thread. There is malice at work here, I can feel it. We owe it to them—"

"Ana," William interjected gently. "We must not speak of this in public. There is much at stake."

"Is there not more at risk in silence?" Ana countered. "If we do not act, who will?" She felt as if she understood the miners, having been locked away for most of her life. At least she had not worried she would suffocate. The miner's terror seemed to fill her with empathy.

"Promise me," she implored, "that you will not dismiss my fears as mere whispers in the wind."

"Never," he assured her. "We will seek the truth. But we must be careful in how we approach the matter."

Ana walked toward the middle of town, knowing that William would be busy for a while making sure the miners were all right. She paused near the general store. Voices, low and urgent, seeped through the walls, and Ana found herself rooted to the spot, an unwilling eavesdropper to a conversation never meant for her ears.

"Can't be natural, all these accidents," came the gruff whisper of a voice she could not place.

"Quiet now," John Thompson's smooth tone cut through. "We're not alone." His words of warning sent a shiver down Ana's spine.

"Too many eyes, too many whispers," the other voice hissed back.

"Careful planning is key," Thompson insisted. "Patience."

Ana's breath hitched. She stepped back, the pieces of a grim puzzle slotting into place with a chilling click.

The weight of suspicion bore down on her. Could the charismatic John Thompson also weave such dark machinations?

She'd heard rumors in her two weeks in Hope Springs. Rumors about why William and John Thompson couldn't seem to see eye to eye. Thompson wanted to turn the town into a destination for the wealthy, closing down all the mines and pushing the men who worked in them out of town. William wanted the town to stay as it was, with everyone welcome.

"William," she murmured to herself. How could she honor the trust he placed in her? She knew she must tell him what she'd overheard.

"Protect," she vowed to the silent night, a promise to the man she loved, to the town she was coming to cherish. With each step back toward the light, her determination grew.

"Thompson," she whispered, the name tasting of ash and betrayal on her tongue. "What are you hiding?"

THE TOWN HALL OF HOPE Springs echoed with discord. Ana Mercer stood against the back wall. The building was filled with townspeople, all voicing their opinion about the incidents in the mines.

"Progress does not come without sacrifice!" John Thompson's voice cut through the murmurs.

Dr. William Mercer countered with equal fervor, "And what of the lives ground to dust beneath your wheels of progress?"

Ana watched as the two men stood at the epicenter of the gathering storm. Her husband's hands, so often tender and healing, now balled into fists of conviction. Thompson stared down the doctor with the arrogance of a man who believed he owned all he surveyed.

"Hope Springs is mine," Thompson spat, his gaze sweeping over the miners whose faces were etched with coal and concern. "I will see it flourish, even if it means dragging it into the future by force."

"Over my dead body," retorted Dr. Mercer.

"Enough," Ana whispered, praying the arguing would end soon.

"Your concern for your pocket outweighs your concern for human life," Dr. Mercer declared.

"Without me, you'd all be nothing but poor dirt farmers!" Thompson retorted.

"Better an honest farmer than a rich tyrant," someone called out from the crowd.

Ana could see the fissures forming among the people she had come to cherish, divisions carved by fear and ambition.

"William," she whispered under her breath. She believed in his cause as much as he did, but she wished he didn't have to be the one to go toe-to-toe with Thompson.

As the meeting descended into chaos, and Ana's resolve hardened. She would stand by her husband, stand by the miners, stand by the truth. She knew the cost might be dear, but some things—justice, love, life itself—were worth the price.

"Thompson," the name again seared her thoughts. He was a puzzle she needed to solve, a shadow that threatened her new life.

The dust had barely settled on the town meeting when Anabelle found herself wandering near the fringes of Hope Springs. She walked to the edge of Thompson's property—a place she'd come to view with a wary eye.

There, in the shadow of the fading sun, she stumbled upon something that quickened her pulse. A leather-bound ledger, half-buried under a pile of discarded timber, its pages fluttering like the wings of a trapped bird. Ana knelt, her fingers brushing against the coarse cover before opening it to the scrawled handwriting within. Each entry was a meticulous record of shipments—not of the silver that brought Hope Springs to life, but of materials unaccounted for, materials that could easily be used to weaken the very structures of the mines.

"Mercy," she whispered. The implications were as clear as they were chilling. In her hand was evidence of deceit, of sabotage.

It was dusk as Ana returned home, the weight of discovery heavy in her hands. She found her sisters, Izzy and Rosie, waiting outside her home for her.

"Ana, what is the matter?" Izzy asked, looking at Ana with confusion.

"Look at this." Ana handed over the ledger, watching as realization dawned on her sisters' faces.

"John Thompson?" Rosie's voice was a fragile thread, laced with disbelief.

"Seems he's been undermining more than just spirits," Ana replied.

"William," Izzy started, her face paling, "what will this mean for him? For all our husbands?"

"I'm not sure," Ana said. "But we cannot let fear dictate our path."

"Nor can we ignore the danger this brings to our doorstep," Rosie added, her gaze locking with Ana's.

"That's true," Ana agreed. "We must tread carefully. We cannot allow such treachery to fester."

"Then we stand with you," Izzy declared, her hand finding Ana's. "As we always have."

"United," Rosie affirmed, completing the circle of hands.

THE FOLLOWING DAY, Ana lingered outside the general store, pretending interest in a display of calico fabric, listening to muffled voices within the store. Two men were speaking about the recent troubles at the mine.

"Accidents they say," one voice chuckled darkly, "yet fortune favors the bold, or so it seems for some."

"True," replied another, a hint of fear tainting his agreement.

Ana moved on, the pieces of the puzzle falling into place within her mind.

At the edge of town, Ana found her opportunity. Old Pete, the livery hand, sat alone on a rickety stool, his eyes downcast.

"Mr. Peterson," Ana began. "May I have a word?"

He looked up, his weathered face a map of reluctance. "Miss Ana, I reckon you should be headin' home 'bout now."

"Please," she implored, taking a tentative step closer, "it's about the accidents at the mine. I believe you've seen something, something important."

Old Pete's gaze darted away. "Ain't right to meddle in folks' affairs," he muttered.

"Nor is it right to turn a blind eye to danger," Ana countered softly. "Think of the families, Mr. Peterson. The children who may grow fatherless should these... 'accidents' continue."

"Miss Ana," he finally said, his voice a hoarse whisper, "it's powerful risky, talkin' 'bout such things."

"More risky to let an innocent town fall prey to one man's ambition," Ana pressed. "You can trust me, Mr. Peterson. Together, we can prevent further harm."

Mr. Peterson's eyes met hers. "I overheard a talk," he began hesitantly, "between Thompson and some outsider. They was arguin' 'bout a shipment, somethin' that didn't go according to plan. Said it would cost too much to fix before the next phase..."

"Next phase?" Ana seized on the phrase, her heart pounding against her ribs like a caged bird seeking freedom. "What next phase?"

"Can't say for sure," Pete admitted, his voice faltering. "But it sounded like whatever's happenin' at the mine ain't finished yet."

"Thank you, Mr. Peterson." Ana placed a reassuring hand on his arm, offering a smile tinged with sorrow. "Your bravery may well save lives."

WHEN ANA ARRIVED HOME, William sat at a small desk, hunched over medical texts.

"William," Ana began.

He looked up, concern etching his features as he took in her pale countenance. "Ana, what is it? You're white as milkweed."

"Thompson," she said. "There's more. I've heard things—ominous, troubling things."

William rose, closing the distance between them with swift strides. His hands found hers. "Tell me everything."

As she recounted the conversation with Mr. Peterson, his grip tightened. Shadows danced across his face, mirroring the turmoil surely roiling within him. "A next phase," William repeated.

"Whatever it is, we can't let it come to pass." Ana's resolve swelled within her chest.

"Agreed." The lines around William's mouth deepened. "But we must proceed with caution. Thompson has the means to bury us should we challenge him unwisely."

"Yet if we do nothing," Ana countered, "Hope Springs itself might be buried under his ambition."

"Perhaps," William murmured, "we could bring this to light at the town meeting. Thompson's machinations could serve as the noose to hang his schemes."

"Public exposure," Ana mused. "It would force his hand, strip away the veneer of respectability…"

"Risky," William admitted, "but less so than letting him keep going with his plans."

"Then it's settled." Ana straightened. "We gather our proof and present it to the people."

"Together," he agreed, pulling her into his embrace. In the circle of his arms, Ana felt the stirrings of hope amidst the fear—a fragile bloom in the frost.

ANA SAT ALONE. SHE leaned over scattered documents, the scent of ink mingling with the mustiness of old paper. She'd spent hours going through papers in the town's archives, trying to learn all she could about the current situation.

Her eyes lingered on a name, etched repeatedly in various ledgers and reports—a whisper of suspicion that had grown into a roar in her mind. The saboteur's identity seemed to be just out of her reach.

Ana rose from her chair. The wooden floorboards creaked beneath her steps as she made her way to William's study.

"William," Ana said, her voice barely above a whisper as she entered the room lined with books and medical instruments. His back was to her, his silhouette framed by the window where the moonlight spilled onto the pages before him.

He turned, his expression a blend of concern and fatigue. "Ana, what is it?"

"I think I know who it is," she said, the words catching slightly in her throat.

"Who?"

"Think about it, William. The accidents, the timing...it's too coincidental," Ana replied, her gaze steadfast. "I believe it's someone with intimate knowledge of the mines—"

"Ana," William interjected. "Be careful before you accuse someone."

"Then what do we do? Sit idly while Hope Springs crumbles?" She refused to let a little fear hurt the community she was growing to love.

"We must consider the repercussions. A wrong move could endanger lives."

"More lives are at stake with every moment we delay!" Ana's words were filled with passion. She wouldn't let anyone be mistreated if she could help them.

"Then we must be certain before we act," William finally said.

"The townspeople," she said, the words spilling out like pebbles into a still pond. "We could seek their help. Many eyes see more than two."

William's expression shifted, his features etched with lines of concern as he considered the proposition. "It's true," he admitted slowly, "the miners, the shopkeepers, they all have pieces to the puzzle. But to share our suspicions..."

"Could lead to panic spreading," Ana finished for him.

"Or worse," he added, his gaze piercing hers with its intensity. "Betrayal. If the saboteur is among them—"

"Then we are already at a disadvantage." Ana's heart hammered against her ribs. The thought of enlisting the town's aid was both beacon and storm; it promised salvation yet threatened destruction.

William stood and paced before the hearth. "To confront the saboteur alone," he murmured, more to himself than to her, "is to risk all in one move."

Ana watched him. "But if we're right," she pressed, the idea a flare in the gloom, "we can end this swiftly."

"Swiftly," he repeated, "and with what cost?" His hands clasped behind his back as he turned away, staring into the fire's dying light.

"Every choice bears a cost," Ana whispered, rising to stand beside him. "We must decide which price we're willing to pay. I know my sisters will help us. Will their husbands?"

William seemed to think about it for a moment. "Yes, I believe they will. Albert is one of the richest men in town, and he shares my vision for it. Charles is the mayor, and he doesn't want things to change either. Yes, they will help us."

"Good." Ana quickly told him more of what she'd found out. "Mr. Jenkins mentioned seeing lantern light by the ridge, well past midnight. None venture there except for..."

William knew what she'd been about to say. "Discreet inquiries," William nodded. "We gather what we can, unseen. We move as the saboteur does."

Ana nodded, agreeing with him.

"Direct confrontation," William's voice broke through the stillness. "It's the only way to end this swiftly, to protect all we hold dear."

"Justice demands it," Ana replied, her hand finding William's, their fingers intertwining as if to draw strength from one another. Their decision was made. Their course set.

"Tomorrow night, we face our foe," William said, his thumb brushing over her knuckles in a comforting gesture.

"Tomorrow," Ana repeated. She wrapped her arms around him. "I can't think of this anymore tonight, William. Let's go to bed."

He blew out the lantern and led her through the quiet house to their bedroom, and that night, Ana learned of the magic Izzy spoke of as she lay in her husband's arms.

After, she rested her head on his chest. "Izzy told me something magic can happen when a woman lays with her husband. Now I know what she meant."

William chuckled softly. "I'll always try to bring magic to your life."

ANA SPREAD THE MAP of Hope Springs on their dining table. "Here," Ana's finger tapped on a junction, "and here." She traced the route. "He'll pass by the old mill at midnight—consistent, if nothing else."

William's eyes followed her motions. "And we shall be his unwelcome shadow," he murmured.

"Let's go over it once more," Ana insisted. She was frightened at the prospect of what they were about to do, but she was used to fear. Her father had taught her all about it.

Ana retrieved a sturdy lantern from the shelf, its metal cold and unyielding beneath her fingers. The chill of it seeped into her skin, a harbinger of the night's embrace that awaited them outside.

William gathered rope and a small, leather-bound journal—their evidence ledger—from the desk. His movements were methodical, each object chosen with precision.

"Ready?" he asked.

"Ready," Ana affirmed. Though her heart hammered within her chest with the fear of what they were about to do, she knew it was the right thing for them and the entire town.

Ana and William stepped out into the night. The town lay still, most of its inhabitants sleeping.

Ana's eyes, wide in the darkness, traced the familiar outlines of buildings they passed. There was no time for fear, only the mission.

William walked beside her. His presence calmed her and made her feel safe.

They neared the spot where they expected the saboteur to strike.

Ana felt every sense sharpen, feeling the faintest shift in the air. They were close now, the moment of truth unfolding before them like the petals of a night-blooming flower.

William reached out, his hand brushing hers in reassurance. It was a simple touch, fleeting yet filled with the promise that they were not alone in this fight. Together, they would face what came.

Ana crouched behind a pile of timber, her body tense as she peered through the gaps. The cold touch of the wood seeped through her thin dress, but it was fear, not chill, that caused her slight shiver. She could hear William's soft breathing from his hiding spot across the way.

She could feel the weight of every passing second. A distant owl hooted and Ana's fingers tightened around the lantern. Her eyes, accustomed to the darkness, flitted from shadow to shadow, searching for any disturbance, any sign of the saboteur.

William shifted slightly. She caught his eye, and he nodded once. Their plan was set. They had only to wait, hearts bound by the silent promise of justice.

Suddenly, the smallest noise—a twig snapping underfoot—sent a jolt through Ana's body. There, emerging from the darkness, was a figure, outlined by the faint glow of the moon. Her breath caught in her throat as the saboteur stepped into view, cloaked in the anonymity provided by the night.

Ana's fingers clenched white-knuckled around the lantern handle, her resolve as steady as her grip. This was the moment they had prepared for, the culmination of all their fears and whispered strategies. The saboteur moved with quiet assurance, unaware of the eyes tracking his every step.

As the dark figure neared the vulnerable point of the mines, Ana knew she couldn't let the past repeat itself.

The saboteur was close now, close enough to see the determination etched in Ana's stance as she readied herself to emerge from the shadows.

The cold night air bit at Ana's cheeks as she and William stepped from the concealing embrace of shadows.

"Stop right there!" William shouted.

The saboteur halted, stiffening as if struck. The identity that unveiled itself beneath the pale moonlight sent a shock through Ana's heart.

"Samuel?" William's tone betrayed a mixture of disbelief and betrayal. The town's kindly blacksmith, a man they had all believed to be a friend, now stood before them cloaked in guilt.

"William, Ana," Samuel murmured. "You don't understand."

Ana's mind raced, flashes of fire and the sounds of splintering wood filled her memory—the destruction he had wrought, now embodied in the man they thought they knew.

"Understand?" Ana's voice trembled with anger and hurt, yet her stance remained firm. "You've endangered every person in Hope Springs."

William reached out, a futile attempt to reason, but Samuel's resolve was shattered. He turned on his heel, and desperation gave way to reckless flight.

"William!" Ana called out, already giving chase. Her skirts billowed behind her, snagging on the roughened edges the unforgiving terrain. She pushed forward, driven by the need to protect, to preserve the life she had come to cherish.

Samuel's figure grew smaller, but Ana's determination swelled with each pounding step. They could not let him slip away into the night, not when so much was at stake.

"Stop, Samuel! Please!" It was a plea wrapped in command, but the blacksmith did not yield. The chase wound through the streets, past homes filled with slumbering dreams, undisturbed by the silent battle waged in their midst.

Ana's breaths came in heavy gasps, her body protesting, yet she willed herself onward.

"Ana, be careful!" William's voice echoed behind her. Yet there was no turning back.

Samuel had vanished into the bowels of the earth, his shadowy form slipping between timeworn beams and trailing dust. Ana's heart hammered against her ribs, a frantic drummer in the quiet symphony of the night.

"Come out, Samuel!" Her voice cut through the silence. There was no response but the distant sound of scuffling feet, drawing her further into the abyss.

Ana pressed on, the narrow tunnels closing in around her. In the flickering light, shadows danced across the jagged rock face.

The path twisted, turned, and dipped, leading her deeper. She stumbled over unseen debris, her skirts catching on splintered wood, her palms grazing cold stone. Still, she persisted, driven by an unyielding spirit that refused to let fear take root.

The tunnel opened into a cavernous chamber. Now, it stood empty, save for two figures locked in a silent struggle—Ana, with the full force of her courage, and the saboteur, cornered at last.

"Enough, Samuel!" Her voice echoed. "You've endangered us all."

His eyes, wide with a feral mix of fear and defiance, met hers. They told a tale of loss, of dreams turned to dust beneath the grindstone of hard living.

"Hope Springs deserves better," she continued. "We could have helped you."

With a roar of thwarted rage, Samuel lunged a final bid for freedom.

But Ana was ready. With agility born of necessity, she sidestepped, her hand shooting out to grasp his arm. Together, they tumbled to the ground, a tangle of limbs and lantern light.

"Let me go!" he spat, struggling against her hold.

"Never." Ana's grip was ironclad. "Not until justice is served."

Ana held him, not with malice, but with the steadfast determination of a woman who had faced down her deepest fears for the sake of others.

"Ana?" It was William.

"Justice will be done," she assured him, her gaze sweeping over the assembled crowd. "Hope Springs will heal."

Dirt clung to their skin, a testament to the ordeal beneath. Ana's breaths came in labored gasps as she and William ascended from the bowels of the earth, their ascent slow but unyielding.

William's hand steadied her when loose stones shifted underfoot. His palm was rough. She felt more than saw his presence beside her.

"Nearly there," William murmured.

They reached the surface. Ana's gaze fell on the mine entrance, its gaping maw a reminder of darkness vanquished. They had faced the abyss together.

Her sisters and their husbands were waiting for them. Charles and Albert each took one of Samuel's arms. "We'll get him to the sheriff," Albert said. "You two need a bath."

Ana looked down at herself and then at William. Her brother-in-law was right. They were filthy.

William's arm wrapped around Ana's shoulders, pulling her close. "You do need a bath," he said, whispering it into her ear.

"Not as much as you do!" she replied, a smile gracing her lips. "Let's go home."

He kissed the top of her head and nodded. "Yes, home. And hopefully by the time we're clean and awake, Samuel will have spilled his story to the sheriff, and he and Thompson will be locked away."

Chapter Seven

William stirred first. Ana's breaths were slow and even beside him, her chest rising and falling with the rhythm of deep sleep. He watched her for a moment, tracing the soft curve of her cheek with his eyes before the weight of reality pressed upon his conscience.

With reluctance stitched into every motion, he slipped from the warmth of the bed. Ana murmured something indecipherable, shifting slightly, and then settled again. He dressed quickly, his mind preoccupied by the events of the night before.

As Ana's consciousness slowly surfaced, she found herself alone in bed. A sigh escaped her lips, and she willed her limbs to move. She dressed in silence, hiding a yawn behind her hand. It was late morning, but it felt as if she'd only slept for an hour or two.

Together, they walked through town. The sheriff's office loomed ahead, a stoic structure that bore witness to the town's trials and tribulations. The door creaked open, and they stepped inside.

Sheriff Dawson was an older man who really shouldn't have still been in office. He looked up from his paperwork, his eyes weary yet vigilant. "Morning, Dr. Mercer, Mrs. Mercer," he greeted, tipping his hat.

"Morning, Sheriff. What news do we have?" William's voice was steady but tinged with the fatigue of the long night.

"Samuel sang like a canary at the crack of dawn," the sheriff said, leaning back in his chair with the creak of aged wood. "Claims he was hired by John Thompson himself to make a mess of those mines."

Ana felt a chill despite the sun beginning to warm the paneled walls. John Thompson was whom they'd suspected all along, and she was glad that he was found out for the rat he was. "Both in custody?" she asked.

"Locked them both up myself. Can't say it was a pleasure, but justice has a way of coming 'round," the sheriff replied, scratching at the stubble on his jaw. His gaze lingered on the couple, recognizing the exhaustion that clung to them.

"Thank you, Sheriff. We'll let you get on with your work," William said, placing a gentle hand on Ana's shoulder, and guiding her toward the exit.

THAT EVENING, THEY walked to Rosie and Charles's modest home. The scent of roasted meat wafted through the air. William ushered Ana up the wooden steps.

"Smells like heaven after a day like today," Ana murmured. They'd had a light lunch, knowing they would be dining with her sisters that evening.

William nodded.

They entered the dining room, greeted by the gentle clatter of cutlery and subdued conversation. Izzy sat beside her husband, poised as ever. Rosie and Charles shared a look, an unspoken understanding passing between them.

"Evening, Ana, William," Charles greeted, rising to offer a firm handshake.

"Evening," William replied, accepting the gesture and taking his place at the table.

Supper unfolded with a tender simplicity, each dish a labor of love from Rosie's skilled hands.

"Justice will find its way here soon," William said softly, breaking the silence that had fallen over the table. "A judge is coming. Two weeks, and we'll see this matter put to rest."

Rosie nodded, her gaze steady. "We've been through so much already. We'll make it through this as well."

Ana listened, her fork tracing patterns in the remains of her meal, her thoughts adrift on the tide of implications. The trial would change things, for better or worse, and she felt the stirrings of apprehension for what lay beyond the gavel's final decree.

"Let's enjoy our time together now," Isabelle suggested. "For all we know, moments like these are the true treasures of life."

Her words, though meant to comfort, hung heavy in the room.

Rosie passed the platter of roasted chicken, the scent of herbs mingling with the warm, yeasty aroma of freshly baked bread. The glow from the oil lamp cast a soft light over the faces gathered around the table, and for a moment, it was easy to forget the events that had occurred.

"Never thought I'd be able to sleep without one eye open again," Charles mused, his fork pausing mid-air. "Feels like we've been living under a shadow for so long."

Ana watched as her sisters nodded in agreement, the relief evident in their weary smiles. They all loved their new town, and they were glad it was safe.

"Hard to imagine just days ago we were all so on edge," Izzy said, her voice barely above a whisper. She looked around the table, her eyes seeking confirmation of this new reality.

The conversation ebbed and flowed with the rhythm of clinking silverware and the occasional laughter. Ana felt the weight of the past months lift slightly with each story told.

As the meal drew to a close, Rosie's brow furrowed in contemplation. She set down her napkin and met Ana's gaze. "But why? Why would anyone want to rid us of the mines? It's our lifeline, after all."

The question hung in the air, raw and unanswered. Ana considered it, her mind sifting through the complexities of greed and ambition that had fueled such treachery. She glanced at William, who sat silently, his expression unreadable in the dim light.

"Sometimes, Rosie," Ana began, her voice steady despite the ache in her chest, "people see only what they stand to gain, not who stands to lose. I hope we never truly understand the hearts of those driven by such darkness," she added.

Silent nods met her statement, a collective understanding passing among them. They were survivors and though the future held no promises, they found comfort in the quiet camaraderie of the present.

William folded his napkin with deliberate care, placing it beside his plate as the room settled into a thoughtful silence.

"John Thompson," William began, his voice a low rumble that resonated within the small dining room, "he sees a different future for Hope Springs. One where opulence and luxury are the cornerstones." He paused, his gaze drifting toward the window as if he could see the town's fate written in the stars. "A town teeming with the affluent, eager to part with their money on fine goods, not the honest sweat of miners."

Ana felt a chill, despite the warmth of the room. There was an unspoken sorrow in William's words. She reached out, her hand finding his, a silent promise of unity.

Charles leaned back in his chair, the leather creaking under his weight. His eyes narrowed, contemplative. "You know," he mused, his voice threaded with a hint of bitterness, "I reckon John can't bear to look upon those miners, each day reminded of what he used to be—one of them, covered in soot and grime."

After the dishes were finished, Charles brought out a deck of cards, and Ana shuffled the deck with deft fingers. She and her sisters had often played card games together while they were in their room back in Massachusetts. It had been a way for them to pass the time.

"Five Card Draw," she declared. Each card landed with precision, a dance of chance and strategy.

They played with laughter and upbeat conversation, enjoying when someone got a lucky card or fooled them all with a bluff. They played until everyone headed to their own homes, knowing they all had to be awake for church in the morning.

THE NEXT MORNING, THE church bell's solemn toll called the town together, its sound reverberating through the crisp mountain air. Inside the whitewashed walls, the pews creaked under the shifting weight of the congregation.

Ana sat beside William, her gaze drifting over the familiar faces. Murmurs filled the sacred space, talk of justice and retribution mingling with prayers of thanks. In the midst of it all stood the preacher, his sermon talking about forgiveness.

After church, the congregants lingered in the churchyard, wanting to talk about what they knew. "Did you hear about Samuel's confession?" one whispered to another, their words a ripple in the pond of their small universe.

"Justice will be served," another affirmed, nodding with the conviction of one who believed deeply in the moral fiber of their community.

William led Ana through the meadow behind the church. They walked in silence, each lost in thought, the tranquility of the day enveloping them in a soft embrace. It was a rare moment of respite, a chance to forget the troubles that were still fresh in their minds.

He picked a wildflower, its petals a delicate blush against the rough backdrop, and tucked it behind her ear. She offered him a smile, faint yet sincere, an acknowledgment of the small joys still to be found. They sat beneath an old oak tree, its branches a testament to the relentless passage of time.

"Days like these," Ana murmured, her voice barely above a whisper, "they make it all seem distant."

"Perhaps that's the gift of nature," William replied, his eyes reflecting the depth of his compassion. "Reminding us that life endures, despite our trials."

They shared a meal of bread and cheese, the simplicity of it grounding them in the present. Laughter bubbled up from somewhere deep within, surprising in its lightness. For a few fleeting moments, they allowed themselves to bask in the serenity that had become so scarce.

The calm shattered with the urgency of a runner's breathless arrival. "Dr. Mercer! Mrs. Freeman—she's in labor!"

With scarcely a glance exchanged, they rose as one. Duty called, and they answered, leaving behind the fleeting sanctuary of the meadow.

In the small confines of the Freeman cabin, sweat beaded on Mrs. Freeman's brow, her face contorted in the pain of childbirth. Ana watched as William's hands worked with practiced ease, guiding new life into the world amidst cries that spoke of both agony and hope. She assisted where she could, her presence a steady anchor in the churning sea of emotion.

It wasn't long before the piercing wail of a newborn filled the room, and relief washed over them all. The baby was healthy and his mother was in good spirits.

"Thank you," Mrs. Freeman whispered, exhaustion lacing her gratitude.

They walked home in silence, the weight of the day settling heavily upon their shoulders.

"William," Ana said at last, her voice cutting through the stillness, "I don't ever want children."

Her words hung between them. He stopped, turning to face her, his expression a blend of understanding and a hint of sadness. There was no judgment in his gaze, only the silent acceptance of her truth and the unspoken promise to carry the burden of it together.

"Ana," he began, but she shook her head gently, forestalling further words.

"Let's just go home," she said.

Chapter Eight

"Never," Ana murmured as she leaned against the side of her house, "I never want children."

Izzy, perched atop a hay bale, her skirts neatly tucked around her, chuckled softly. A wisp of her hair caught in the sunlight as she shook her head. "Oh, Ana," she said, "you'll change your mind." There was assurance in her voice, born not from naivety but from a sister's intimate knowledge.

Rosie, sitting cross-legged on the ground, braiding stems of grass into intricate patterns, didn't look up. Her hands moved with practiced ease, and her voice held the practicality that grounded them all. "A dozen," she stated simply. "That's what I want. A dozen children."

Ana shuddered. "You didn't see a baby's birth. You have no idea of how impossible the whole situation is!"

Izzy shrugged. "Women do it all the time."

"That doesn't make it easier!" Ana said, shaking her head. "Anyway, I was hoping you two would help me make a meal for the Freeman family. She shouldn't ever have to walk again after what she's been through!"

When her sisters readily agreed, Ana led them into the house.

Ana's hands moved in quiet harmony with those of her sisters, the rhythm of chopping and stirring a soothing cadence amidst the clatter of pots and the hiss of the stove. The kitchen was warm, a sanctuary against the briskness of the early evening as they prepared a meal meant to comfort.

"More salt," Rosie murmured. She tended to the stew with a gentle stir, her movements unhurried.

Izzy hummed softly as she sliced bread with deft precision.

They bundled the meal with care, wrapping the bread in a cloth and ladling the stew into a pot that could keep the warmth inside. The Freemans' home was not far, but the sisters walked in purposeful silence, the weight of their offering a shared burden between them.

"Mrs. Freeman will be grateful for this," Izzy said as they reached the doorstep, her eyes reflecting the last glimmers of dusk.

"I'm sure she will," Ana replied.

They left the meal with soft words and softer smiles, retreating from the threshold of beginnings back into the night's embrace.

As they walked away, Ana couldn't stop thinking about how happy Mrs. Freeman had looked with her child in her arms. She didn't seem to be looking at the boy and thinking about the pain she'd gone through to get him. Maybe it was worth it for her.

"Remember when Mama would tell us about the day we were born?" Rosie asked, breaking the silence.

Izzy nodded. "Three little babies, all at once. She made it sound so...magical."

Ana's steps faltered momentarily, her heart tightening at the thought. "How did she do it?" she whispered, more to herself than to her sisters. "Three babies crying, needing, all at once..."

Rosie's hand found Ana's, a silent anchor in the night. "She had us," she said simply. "And Mother loved us in a way that is stronger than the pain she went through to have us."

"Today," Ana began, "I think I understood what Mama meant. What you said, Izzy. About magic." She folded herself into an armchair, the fabric whispering secrets of days past.

Izzy's eyes softened, a smile tugging at the corner of her lips. Rosie, seated on a worn rug by the fire, looked up, a question in her gaze.

"It was there, in Mrs. Freeman's eyes. Amidst the pain and fear...there was wonder." Ana's breath hitched. "Life, coming forth from another. It's a kind of enchantment, isn't it?" Her hands traced circles along the arms of the chair, seeking solace in the rhythm.

"So much magic," Izzy agreed, smiling.

Rosie nodded slowly. "Speaking of wonders," she said, "Charles kissed me today."

"Finally," Izzy exclaimed, a laugh lilting in her voice.

"Was it..." Ana hesitated, choosing her words with care, "...everything you hoped?"

"More," Rosie confessed, cheeks flushing with the admission. "There is a tenderness between us now. A fondness that feels like it's been growing, quiet and steady, just beneath our awareness."

"Like roots entwining beneath the soil," Ana mused softly.

"Exactly." Rosie's affirmation was a gentle exhalation, her smile warming the room.

The sun dipped low, casting a golden hue over the small kitchen as Ana set two plates on the worn table. William's footsteps echoed on the wooden porch outside before he pushed open the door, a gust of evening air swirling around him as he entered.

"Evening," he greeted with a tired smile, his medical bag landing with a soft thud by the door.

"Supper's ready," Ana said. She watched him wash up at the basin, his hands methodical and sure—a contrast to the storm of thoughts in her head.

As they sat down to a meal of stewed beef and fresh bread, the silence was comfortable. Ana broke it first, her fingers fidgeting with the edge of her napkin.

"I spoke to Izzy and Rosie today," she began.

"Ah?" William propped his elbows on the table, his attention fully on her now. "And how are they?"

"Rosie's glowing," Ana replied, a faint smile touching her lips. "She and Charles—well, they're finding their way to each other."

"Good, good." His nod was absentminded.

"And Izzy...she made light of it, but we talked about the birthing yesterday. It was..." Ana's voice faltered, the memory vivid in her mind. "It was difficult."

He reached across, covering her hand with his. "Childbirth can be. But you were there for Mrs. Freeman, and that's what matters."

Ana drew in a deep breath, the exhale shaky. "William, do you think less of me if I admit I'm scared of having children?"

"Scared?" The concern in his eyes was clear, unfeigned. "Ana, whatever is on your mind, you can tell me."

She met his gaze then. "I do want them—children, I mean. Someday." A sigh escaped her, carrying the weight of her confession. "But the idea of childbirth terrifies me. To be so out of control, the pain..."

"Ana." His voice was a balm, soothing the raw edges of her fears. "You don't have to decide anything now. And when the time comes, should you wish it, I'll be right there with you. You won't be alone."

After finishing the dishes, Ana joined William in his office. William sat ensconced behind his desk, spectacles perched on the bridge of his nose as he pored over medical journals, their pages dense with knowledge that promised solace to the suffering.

Ana curled in a corner of the settee, her fingers tracing the well-worn spine of *Little Women* before flipping it open. The words of Louisa May Alcott, though familiar and comforting, struggled to hold her full attention. Her mind wandered through the prose, lost amidst the March sisters' trials and triumphs, seeking parallels in her own life.

Their mother had gotten a copy of the book when she and her sisters were younger, and it had become an instant favorite for her, Rosie, and Izzy. They'd read it over and over, and even acted out one of the plays Jo was always writing. Their mother had applauded madly.

As night deepened, the book fell gently from Ana's lap, and she glanced up to find William still immersed in his studies.

"Bedtime," she whispered, more to the room than to him.

In the privacy of their bedroom, the weight of the world slipped from their shoulders. His hands were tender, and knowledgeable, weaving a warmth that spread through her veins. She surrendered to the sensation, to the magic he conjured with each caress.

"William," she breathed, as the space between them vanished, "even if I didn't want children, I don't think I could stop...this...with you."

He responded not with words but with a kiss.

After, tendrils of William's breath fanned against Ana's skin. His chest rose and fell in a slow rhythm, lulling her into a state of half-awareness. She lay still, listening to the sound of slumber that escaped him. The moonlight wove through the curtains, casting a pale glow over his features.

The room was steeped in tranquility, the world outside their door a distant memory. Here, time seemed to tread lightly, allowing moments to linger, thoughts to unfurl like the petals of a blooming rose. As the minutes trickled by, Ana felt a warmth spreading from her chest, an ember of emotion glowing brighter with each shared heartbeat.

A sigh escaped her, a whisper lost amidst the symphony of nighttime sounds. The realization settled within her like the final piece of a puzzle long left incomplete. She was falling in love with William Mercer, not out of necessity or convenience, but because he had become the compass point of her existence, the unexpected joy in a life she thought mapped by duty alone.

Yet as the certainty of her affection swelled, she worried that he had no feelings for her beyond those of lust. She suddenly wasn't sure if it was enough to keep them together.

Chapter Nine

Ana joined Dr. William Mercer in the infirmary every morning, before spending the afternoons with her sisters. It felt good to be helping her husband but still being allowed to spend a few hours every day with her sisters. Slowly she was getting used to spending time away from her sisters, though it was much harder than missing their mother. Mother had given them as much time as she could, but her evenings had been with Father. She and her sisters had rarely not been in the same room together.

William moved with ease among the patients in the waiting room. Ana watched him, feeling the weight of responsibility on her shoulders—the same weight he bore with such grace.

Ana listened to the soft groans of the ill. Each morning unfolded like the pages of a well-worn journal, details penned in the careful script of routine.

"Hand me the bandages, please," William said.

Ana complied, her fingers brushing against his as she passed the linen strips. Their eyes met briefly. In these shared glances, she found affirmation of her growing skills and a kinship born from serving side by side.

They moved from patient to patient, a dance of compassion choreographed by necessity. She applied salves with delicate precision, wrapped wounds with newfound confidence, and offered soothing words that she hoped might ease more than physical pain. William observed her progress, his nods more telling than any spoken praise.

Ana had never had any desire to be a nurse, but she found she was good at it, and she enjoyed it more than she could express. She didn't know if she simply liked working with her husband or the nursing itself, but either way, she enjoyed the time she spent in the infirmary.

The infirmary buzzed with life. Miners with coughs, children with scrapes earned in youthful exuberance; women worn thin by the rigors of frontier existence—they all came and went, their stories etching themselves into Ana's soul.

With each passing day, her hands grew surer, her resolve firmer. She learned the language of healing, of caring by watching William, who saw healing as more of an art than a science.

When the clock signaled the end of her morning vigil, Ana would bid farewell to the infirmary and its occupants. She often told stories of her mornings to her sisters in the afternoons, but she was always careful not to give any names or descriptions of people because that felt unethical to her.

THE NEEDLES DANCED between their fingers, threads weaving bonds as tight as the stitches in the linen. Ana, Izzy, and Rosie sat in a circle, surrounded by the soft hum of afternoon light. Their conversations meandered through the complications and joys of married life.

"Albert becomes more distant with each ledger he buries himself in," Isabelle's voice was a whisper.

"Charles's ambitions stretch far beyond the mountains," Rosabelle added, her tone touched by the shadow of doubt, "sometimes I worry he'll take me away from here. From the two of you."

Ana listened to her sisters and offered advice when it was asked for. Though she knew no more of marriage than either of them.

ANA HELD A WOMAN'S hand, calloused from years of toil, as life burst forth in a cry—a cry soon echoed by another. Twin boys, their arrival doubling the joy in the room. Ana watched, her emerald eyes reflecting a kindred fascination. She knew the bond of sharing a womb.

Later, when the new mother rested and the twins lay swaddled side by side, Ana lingered. She traced the delicate features of the newborns. In the quiet of the infirmary, Ana felt the weight of many lives—those lost, those just beginning.

She thought of her Mother, her absence an ever-present pang in Ana's chest. The pain was a dull blade, but standing there, watching over these new souls, she found solace. It was as if each delivery, each tiny heartbeat, filled the empty spaces left behind.

Dim candlelight flickered across the modest supper table as Ana set down her fork, the metal tines chiming faintly against the porcelain.

"Ana," William began, "I must commend you. The aptitude you've shown in the infirmary—it's quite remarkable."

She looked up, meeting his eyes. "Thank you, William," she replied, her words floating like leaves on a still pond. "I appreciate how patient you are with me. I could never learn without your guidance."

"Perhaps," he conceded. "But a fine nurse needs more than just instruction. She needs intuition and compassion...You have both."

Ana felt a flush of pride warming her cheeks. "Thank you for saying so."

THE NEXT MORNING, AS the sun cast long shadows over Hope Springs, Izzy wandered into the infirmary, her face pale. Her hand rested on her abdomen, a subtle cradle for her discomfort.

"Ana," she murmured, her voice lacking its usual vivacity. "My stomach... it's been turning all morning."

"Let's have you lie down," Ana said. She guided Izzy to a cot.

As Izzy settled with a quiet groan, Ana's thoughts drifted to the many women she'd seen in these beds. There was a silent kinship among them, a shared vulnerability that transcended the walls of the infirmary.

"William will know what to do," Ana reassured her sister, though her own heart thrummed with trepidation. "Rest now. I'm here."

Izzy nodded, her eyelids fluttering like moth wings before succumbing to their weight. Ana watched over her. She cared about all of her patients, but her concern for Izzy was strong.

The infirmary door swung open with a gentle nudge from William's shoulder, his arms occupied by an assortment of glass vials and cotton bandages. The sunlight filtered through the windows, casting a somber glow on Izzy's pallid face. Ana had never seen her sister so still, so fragile beneath the white sheets.

"Ana, could you help me with these?" William asked. Ana nodded, her hands moving mechanically to assist him.

"Thank you," he said. "Izzy, tell me what's wrong."

While William talked with and examined her sister, Ana felt a chill run down her spine, her fingers tightening around a glass vial. She knew the signs, had learned to read them as well as any book. But knowing did not quell the dread that rose within her like floodwater.

"You're expecting," William announced, a gentle smile softening the gravity of his words.

Izzy's breath hitched, her hand fluttering to her abdomen in disbelief. Ana's heart ached at the sight, the joy and fear warring on her sister's face.

"Expecting?" Izzy echoed, her voice barely above a whisper.

"Yes," William confirmed, placing a comforting hand on her shoulder. He spoke of new life with reverence, yet Ana's mind raced with thoughts of the birthings she'd witnessed—the screams, the sweat, the blood.

"Congratulations," Ana murmured, the word feeling like a stone on her tongue. She smiled, but it didn't quite reach her eyes.

"Thank you, Ana." Izzy's gaze met hers, seeking solace in shared understanding. "I must tell Rosie."

THAT AFTERNOON AS THE triplets sat together in Ana's parlor, Izzy looked at Ana and then sighed. "Rosie, I need to talk to you," Izzy said.

"Of course," Rosie replied, setting aside her sewing. "What is it?"

"I'm...We're going to have a baby. Albert and I." Izzy's voice trembled.

Rosie's eyes widened, a myriad of emotions flickering within. "Oh, Izzy, that's wonderful!"

"Is it?" Izzy bit her lip, the uncertainty gnawing at her. "Albert has never spoken of wanting children. And after all the births Ana has seen..."

"Shh," Rosie soothed, reaching across the space between them to squeeze Izzy's hand. "He loves you. This will bring you even closer."

"I hope you're right." Izzy attempted a smile.

Ana watched from the doorway, her fears mirrored in Izzy's cautious hope.

"We need to start sewing for the baby then, don't we?" Ana asked, smiling. She loved the idea of making something special for her future niece or nephew.

A plaintive wail pierced the hum of conversation. Ana turned, her eyes narrowing as she sought the source. The sound came again, a baby's cry, insistent and raw. Without a word, she rose.

She reached the door, the coolness of the handle seeping into her palm. There, on Ana and William's porch, bundled in coarse blankets, lay an infant. Its face was ruddy, its tiny fists punching the air with the ferocity of its cries.

Ana knelt, the hem of her skirt collecting dust from the boards. Her breath caught as she took in the sight, the enormity of what lay before her dawning slowly. She extended a trembling hand, her fingertips brushing the soft down of the baby's cheek. The crying ceased for a heartbeat, curious eyes locking onto hers.

"Who would leave you here?" she murmured, more to herself than the child. The baby's gaze held a depth that seemed impossible for one so young.

Ana gathered the infant into her arms, the warmth of its small body seeping through the layers of fabric. She stood, cradling the bundle close, her mind churning.

As she held the baby, the silence of the house behind her felt suddenly profound. The sisters' laughter and chatter had ceased, and Ana knew they were watching, waiting for her to turn back with answers she did not possess. She gazed down at the child, feeling its steady heartbeat against her own, their lives momentarily entwined by circumstance.

For a moment, Ana closed her eyes, taking in the scent of the infant. There was nothing quite like the smell of a new baby. When she opened her eyes, resolve hardened within her.

"Let's go inside," she whispered. Her heart was heavy with questions, but she carried the child with tenderness.

William's familiar footsteps approached the front porch. Ana paced back and forth, the baby nestled in the crook of her arm, its cries piercing the quiet twilight. She felt each wail as a sharp tug at her heart. Her sisters had gone home to prepare supper for their husbands, and she was left alone with the baby.

"William," she said, her voice strained with worry as he crossed the threshold. He removed his hat, revealing furrowed brows that smoothed upon laying eyes on the pair.

"Let's see here," William said softly. "We can try infant food. It's better if a baby is fed by breast, but I do have some infant food in the infirmary. It's gentle on the stomach. I'll run and get some and will be back in ten minutes."

True to his word, he came back a short while later, carrying a can of something.

Ana watched him with a mixture of relief and doubt as he set about preparing a bottle with practiced hands. The baby's cries subsided to fitful whimpers, and it latched onto the makeshift teat with an instinctive hunger. In that moment, Ana's restless pacing ceased, and she allowed herself a silent breath of reprieve.

In the days that followed, they made inquiries throughout Hope Springs, their voices growing hoarse with the repetition of the question: "Do you know this child?" Yet, the town's response was a resounding murmur of uncertainty. Each shake of the head, each shrug of the shoulders added another layer to the mystery enfolding the baby girl.

With the dawn of each new morning, Ana's routine encompassed the dual roles of nurse and caretaker. While her hands were busy with bandages and balms in the infirmary, her mind wandered to the little being swaddled in her sisters' care. Her sisters, who chattered about their husbands and stitched together quilts, now also whispered soft lullabies to the foundling cradled in their arms.

It became a rhythm of sorts—a dance between duty and devotion. And as the baby's cries grew less frequent, replaced by coos and gurgles, Ana felt a bond forming, fragile and unspoken, but as real as the weight of the child in her arms each night.

A WEEK HAD PASSED, each day closing with the same unanswered questions. The baby's origins remained a mystery, and Hope Springs had offered no claim to the infant. In the quiet of the parlor, Ana sat by the firelight, the child nestled against her chest, her eyes tracing the gentle rise and fall of the tiny form.

"William," Ana said, "we've searched and asked tirelessly. No one claims the baby." She looked at her husband, saying a silent prayer he had come to the same conclusion she did.

"Then it seems," he said with a weighted pause, "she is ours now."

The words hung between them—a shared understanding. Ana nodded, the corners of her mouth curving upward in a tender smile. It was an unorthodox blessing, a gift they hadn't sought but had been bestowed upon them, nonetheless.

"Ours," she repeated. A laugh, light and airy, escaped her as she confessed, "I'm thrilled, truly. To think, I have a baby—without the pains of childbirth."

William's chuckle mingled with her own. Her heart swelled with an affection for a child she had not borne yet felt intrinsically connected to.

In the flicker of the fireplace, the baby cooed, oblivious to the depth of the conversation, to the life-changing decisions being made over her slumbering head. Ana watched her, the joy of unexpected motherhood blooming within her chest, as William's presence anchored her to this new reality they would navigate together.

Ana cradled the infant, her movements gentle and assured. Shadows crossed William's face as he watched them.

He cleared his throat, the sound cutting through the stillness. "Ana," he began. "The joy this little one brings...it's more than I could have imagined."

She glanced up, meeting his gaze. There was a vulnerability there she had not seen before.

"Yet," he continued, his eyes never leaving hers, "it stirs in me a longing—a sorrow for the children I'll never call my own." His words were soft, but they landed heavily in the space between them.

Ana felt a pang in her chest. "William," she whispered. Her heart ached for him, for the dreams that seemed just out of reach. "I'll think more about it."

Chapter Ten

Ana's fingers moved deftly, her needle piercing the fabric, joining blue and red squares into a patchwork of warmth meant for Lillian. They called her Lilli more often than not, but they all loved her.

Rosie sat across from Ana, her hands just as busy, but her eyes often drifting to the cradle where the baby slept.

Izzy folded diapers for the baby.

"Blue like the sky," Ana murmured, holding up a square. "Red like the roses by the well." She smiled but it was a weary one, the corners of her mouth betraying the effort it took. The colors blurred before her eyes. Between the mornings in the infirmary, and the nights filled with Lilli's feedings, she was exhausted.

"Perfect for our Lilli," Isabelle responded.

"She'll love it," Rosabelle added.

Ana let out a sigh, her thoughts trailing off to William. He would wrap this quilt around his child, she knew, with the same tenderness he had shown her. Ana wished she had a way to take some of the burden from him, but she didn't know how beyond helping him in the infirmary every morning.

Lilli stirred, a tiny fist breaking free from the blanket's embrace. Ana stilled her sewing, watching as her sisters paused until the baby settled once more.

"Almost done," Ana said.

Rosie looked down at the quilt and smiled. "We'll have to make another when we finish this one. Izzy's baby needs one too."

"And I think we'll need one more after Izzy's," Ana said softly. "I haven't told William yet, so don't say a word!"

"Is this a good thing?" Rosie asked softly.

"William wants children," Ana murmured, the needle pausing at the crest of a blue square. "He loves Lilli so much, but he wants his own children."

She looked over at the sleeping baby in the cradle. "It was Lilli," Ana continued. "Deciding to keep her... It stirred something in him. A longing."

Her fingers resumed their work, but more slowly now. She could feel her sisters' eyes on her, their brows furrowed with concern and curiosity alike.

"I fear it, though," she confessed. "Childbirth. The pain it brings." She glanced toward the cradle where Lilli lay, peaceful in dreams. "I love her, dearly so. But to endure such agony...Can I love another who would cause it?"

In the periphery, she sensed her sisters exchanging looks, their own concerns about childbirth etched into the lines around their eyes.

"Ana," Rosie said gently, reaching out to cover her hand with her own. "It's a love different from any other. A love that grows, even through pain."

"Besides," Izzy said with a smile, "you've already proven you're stronger than you think."

Ana's sisters converged upon her, their arms enfolding her in an embrace that spoke of shared joy and unyielding support.

"Then we sew not just for Lilli," Rosie whispered, "but for the little ones yet to come."

"And you'll love them," Izzy added, her tone firm, "as fiercely as you love us."

"Love is infinite, Ana," Rosie said, "it multiplies with every heartbeat."

THE CLINK OF SILVERWARE against porcelain had faded, leaving the room draped in a quiet that mirrored the night sky outside. Ana cradled Lilli in her arms, the soft suckling the only sound punctuating the silence.

William sat across from her, his eyes tracing the tender scene.

"William," Ana's voice was almost a whisper. "There is something I must tell you."

He leaned forward.

"I believe... I am with child." The words tumbled out, half fear, half wonder.

The room seemed to hold its breath, waiting as William processed her confession. Then his face lit up with a smile that warmed her.

"Truly?" He was obviously thrilled. "Ana, that is... that is wonderful news!"

She watched him rise and come around the table to where she sat, still feeding Lilli. His hands, those healers' hands, were steady as they rested on her shoulder, grounding her.

"To have a child of my own," he said, "to love as I do Lilli..." He paused, his eyes shining with unshed tears. "And for that child to come from you, the woman I love, it's more than I ever dared hope for."

Ana felt a swell of something inside her. It was overwhelming and yet, at this moment, it was right. She could not fathom the future, but she knew that whatever came, it would be theirs to face together.

"William," she murmured, her hand finding his. "I *am* scared, but your joy...it helps."

The silence between them stretched. Ana's heart hitched as she regarded William, the lines of his face softened by candlelight. His words lingered in the air, tender yet terrifying in their implications.

"Love is not a debt you owe for carrying a child," she whispered.

William's smile didn't falter, but it deepened with an earnestness that tugged at her soul. "Ana," he said. "I do not say it out of obligation."

His hand, once resting on her shoulder, now cradled her cheek. "I say it because it's the truth. It was true before this news and it will remain true."

Ana searched his eyes. Her breath caught as the reality of his words sank in, roots entwining with the very core of her being.

"Less than a year apart," he continued. "Our home filled with the sounds of two little ones."

Ana looked down at the baby in her arms. "I hope this one is sleeping through the night before the next one arrives."

He chuckled. "I do too. Nothing could have made me happier than this news, Ana. I hope you know that."

She smiled, nodding. "I'm getting used to the idea."

Ana put the baby in her cradle before joining William in the bedroom where he waited for her.

Ana's fingers trembled as she reached for William's outstretched hand. "William," she began. "I..."

The words lodged in her throat. She swallowed hard, trying to force the words. Even though he'd admitted he loved her, she was having a hard time saying the same thing to him. Yet as she gazed into his eyes, those wellsprings of unwavering resolve, she found a reflection of her longing—a yearning not just for the comfort of companionship but for the all-consuming blaze of love that threatened to consume her.

"I love you," she said, the declaration slipping out like a sigh carried on the evening breeze.

His smile was slow, deliberate as if he was savoring her words. There was no triumph in his expression, only a deep-seated contentment that spoke of shared hardships and the solace found in each other's presence.

"Ana," he replied, "you've given me more than I ever dared hope for."

Epilogue

Ana cradled the weight of new life in each arm, the tiny breaths of her twin sons whispering against her skin. Seven months had scarcely passed since Lilli's first cries pierced the silence of their world, and now these two—her boys—lay nestled against her.

"William," she said, her voice barely above the gentle hum of the parlor, "two at once. I will never understand how my mother managed with three!"

Her gaze found his, saw the shimmer of unshed tears. "Ana," he started, but words failed him, surrendering to something far more profound than speech.

She smiled. Her heart was a vessel filled to the brim—not with trepidation as it once had been—but with an overwhelming love that threatened to spill over.

"William," Ana began again, "I want a houseful. A couple dozen little feet and laughter." She paused, watching the twins squirm, their tiny fists flailing with innocent vigor. "But perhaps not all at once."

He chuckled, the sound mingling with the soft coos of their sons. Stepping forward, William leaned down, pressing a kiss to her forehead, one to each baby's downy head.

"Whatever you wish," he whispered. "We'll fill this house with life and love, and take each day as it comes."

Ana nodded. She now understood why women who'd had children were happy to have more. These little creatures, a mix of her and William, were already filling her heart with joy. Just like their sister, Lilli. And while she couldn't count on more children arriving on her doorstep, nothing could keep her from having more.

"Then let's begin with these two," she said, her eyes never leaving the twins' peaceful slumber. "Let's fill our lives with the laughter of our children and the warmth of our love."

ANA SAT IN THE SAME parlor where she had once sewn quilts for Lilli, the walls echoing with the laughter of her children—a chorus of joy that filled the spaces once hollowed by fear.

Lilli was out walking with the man she hoped to spend her life with. Her sisters and their families would be there for supper. Together, they would spend time with the people most precious to them.

"More than I ever dared hope for," she murmured, tracing the lines on William's face, etched by time and smiles.

"Oh yes," William agreed, his hand covering hers, warm and steady as ever. "And yet, here we are."

"Here we are," Ana said with a smile.